DEMIGODS ON SPEEDWAY

DEMIGODS ON SPEEDWAY

AURELIE SHEEHAN

THE UNIVERSITY OF
ARIZONA PRESS

TUCSON

The University of Arizona Press
www.uapress.arizona.edu

Printed in the United States of America
19   18   17   16   15   14   6   5   4   3   2   1

Cover design by Leigh McDonald

Library of Congress Cataloging-in-Publication Data
Sheehan, Aurelie, 1963–
 [Short stories. Selections]
 Demigods on speedway / Aurelie Sheehan.
    pages cm.
 Summary: "A collection of linked short stories set in modern-day Tucson, Arizona,
featuring characters who struggle to make ends meet, find love, and find meaning in re-
cession-era America. The characters are players in a contemporary southwestern story
that draws from tropes and characters in Greek mythology"—Provided by publisher.
 ISBN 978-0-8165-3110-3 (pbk. : alk. paper)
 1. Short stories, American. I. Title.
 PS3569.H392155D46 2014
 813'.54—dc23
                    2014000132

♾ This paper meets the requirements of ANSI/NISO Z39.48-1992 (Permanence of
Paper).

For Reed

*When young Dawn with her rose-red fingers shone
once more, the gods awoke. They dressed with a
decent sense of casual chic and spoke in human tongue.*

Contents

DEMIGODS ON SPEEDWAY

JOURNEY

Olympus Falls

"My city is in danger. It's out of hand, we're overrun—the dealers coming up from Mexico and the lazy sons of bitches sending their lazy sons of sons of bitches to our schools, and now what am I seeing? Here's something new: Africans. I'm not talking brown, these are *black* people, real native types, headdresses, pregnant, carrying children, dragging children— the men like this guy, tall son of a bitch, a black tree, a Halloween tree. His face is shining—he's just standing there—gangly arms, wicked plans. He's just standing at the bus stop, waiting for our fine American transportation system to come pick him up, pick up his harem, bring them somewhere— where? Wherever they go. To the courthouse to plead for mercy. Muslims now, too, just waiting. Waiting for an opportunity. And I have no fucking idea how they got in."

Zero turns off the voice recorder and lets it drop to his lap, a thoughtful half measure, and then he places it back in the shallow reservoir by the cup holder and accelerates out of the intersection at Fifth, continuing north on Alvernon toward Speedway. His car is sleek and soft, and he's inside, in the belly of a cat, isolated and insulated from lesser Tucson. The seventy-one-degree microclimate, preset; the sixteen-way seat angle and lumbar support, preset; the semianiline baby-skin leather of the seats and armrests and the blood-brown, walnut-trimmed steering wheel and shift knob and console; the music coming from the Mark Levinson audio system with the nineteen well-placed speakers—*nineteen* speakers!—being the excellent world music CD his wife, Hanna, left in (not all that excellent really). *World Music for Dummies* she called it, he now remembers, as he listens to another minute of paranoid howling, considering all the while that he could speak, halt the madness, return to silence—or even to another, *any* other, of the CDs his wife or son or daughter have given him. But he leaves this on for now. And so, motoring past a medical lab and then one of Tucson's ubiquitous beaten-down apartment buildings, this one called Oasis Palms, he is listening to a Senegalese chant, soon replaced by the insanely sexy non-woman in the car's navigation system, who says: "Approaching Speedway Boulevard, alternate route." Though he's well aware of how to get home, Zero has left on, as is his habit, the navigation system. He finds pleasure in its—in her—company. He calls her Quiet Woman, in certain and complete contrast to Hanna. Quiet Woman tends to the information and potential information at his finger-tips, at his voice's command. Directions, music, climate control. All exist-ing for him alone: a purr of compliance and domination. He enjoys his commute, the half hour or forty minutes to Raytheon and back, longer if it includes forays to Anthony's or Ghost Fish Grill for drinks or din-ner, with women who are mere mortals, women who come and go, unlike Zero himself, whose life has seemed by all accounts never ending, power-ful. "Eject disk," he says, convulsing.

He warms when he thinks of her, Alyssa, she of the long neck and black hair like a dangling stole and most of all, that ass. An ass of mytho-logical proportions! Smutty, yes, completely so, and huge and beautiful, the flesh soft, stuffed into pants or a pencil skirt. He first noticed Alyssa two weeks ago at a team-building seminar with Communications and Immigration Control and Identity Management. She's got the ass, and she's smart as a button. But it's not the button-like intelligence nor the ass he's thinking of at this particular moment (5:21 p.m., 105° outside, 71° inside), it's the wide, flat expanse from hip to hip, and then—as if he's scanning a photograph—that ever-so-slight bow to her legs. He overlikes it, this imperfection. It's almost ugly, but exquisite when paired with the rest of the package, the sleekness and sexiness and theoretical profession-alism. It's a plea of some kind, for mercy? Definitely an invitation. He ex-periences it as a form of violence, his desire for Alyssa. At the team-build-ing seminar, she was wearing a lemon-yellow suit with a black camisole. She's about thirty, he thinks. Married? Not that it matters. This is what was said at the proverbial water cooler, a midmeeting break with bottled water from Fiji and muffins and fruit: "You have a way with words, Alyssa. I'm impressed." And she flapped her hands in a sweet, small gesture, nervous and not nervous, nervous but owning up to the feeling and thus neutraliz-ing it. He nodded as she chattered on about her education, the two years she'd been with the company—how much she loved it, how much of a hard-nosed guy Allan was, but also a fine guy underneath. He imagined how it would be to lift the straight skirt from the narrowness above her knees, over her bowed, nearly ashamed thighs, and then above the plump bump of that ass.

"Call Ram Stern, mobile," says Zero, out of the silence of his perfect airtight enclosure—the Senegalese chanting had been unnerving really, you'd call that music?—and the automobile complies, Quiet Woman and her minions. "Calling Ram Stern, mobile." Ram Stern is not in. "Ram, uh," says Zero, "re: the call with IMAP, some follow-up questions. One, I think you erred by allowing Randall to gloss over the funding issues in the second quarter. He oversteps, chronically now. This cannot fucking happen. His enthusiasm's going to come back and bite us in the ass. Legal minefield, Ram, you know this. Let's get our ducks in a row here before the meeting, all right? Tonight, tomorrow at the latest. Thank you, Ram." And click. "Ending call," says Quiet Woman. A Chinese restaurant the size of China itself looms up—a green, cement-block warehouse with a red pagoda. On the other side of Speedway: another bus stop, another group of ne'er-do-wells. Zero shakes his head, simultaneously of the world and unequivocally, exceptionally removed from it. If he thinks of himself at all, his corporeal form, it's as a highly functioning machine, a conduit of divine elegance, with which he has sought and absorbed plentiful harvests of information, of *knowledge*, and alchemically changed this knowledge into action, well-considered and well-targeted, responding to the world and its requirements. He creates something from nothing, wealth from scratch. It's a habit now, almost a physical need. His wife doesn't understand, not fully—but then, no one does. Hanna, who is in Phoenix today for blood work and will stay the night at the Chartreuse Retreat & Spa, finding at check-in a "Queen's Key," a specially wrapped box, as Zero's secretary described it to him, offered with a rose. Inside the box is a silver key representing an open ticket to the spa, carte blanche on facials and stone massages and microdermabrasions and all the other services that women enjoy. In about a block, Zero will pass, actually, the clinic where technicians first discovered the lump, though he will not recognize the building, having never been there. He was the one to convince her to go to Phoenix (two hours north at ninety miles an hour on I-10) for medical treatment, the best care in the region. The commute is a difficulty, of course, but the spa will offer some solace, and she can stay as often as she likes, as many nights as she likes. "We'll get through this together," he murmured when she first told him. "I'll see to everything." He takes pride in his verbal prowess, his ability to smooth things over. Zero leans abruptly forward, casting a look all around as if he's searching for something, or taking in all that he usually almost ignores, or does ignore.

This thirteen-mile stretch from south to north, from the industrial center where Raytheon lords, to the Tucson Foothills where the lords build homes, is a desert to him. It's ironic that the middle of this city, with the dumpy apartment buildings, half-assed strip malls, riffraff of all kinds, would be more of a desert than the *actual* desert—the Sonoran wilderness that surrounds Tucson, a ring of mountain ranges dense with saguaros and javelinas—which, after all, one can hike in, bike through. (Rising above the Walgreens sign and a billboard for auto insurance loom the ostentatious Catalinas, but there are also the Rincons, the Tucsons, and the Santa Ritas.) Central Tucson—or for that matter South Tucson, the Mexican side of town—is desert in the classic, cartoonish sense of the word. Nothing living, nothing that matters. Who lives at Oasis Palms or Regency Court or Sunrise Gardens? Truly nobody. At Oasis Palms alone, sixty units full of nobody. On the corner, a nobody in a cape waving a sign, lunging at him now.

"It's not that I'm against these men," he says into the recorder. "Men are men. Men have essential qualities no matter where they're from—no matter how lunatic their religions or barbaric their countries. If you had the time and money, you could train them. We must think for others; not everyone can think for themselves. We're falling into laziness as a country. Tucson is just one example, I think, of how things can go wrong. The men here—these people"—and here Zero actually gestures to the world outside his car—"may be, at least some of them, citizens. We have a responsibility toward them." Click off. On again. "Remind me to send the Lufthansa model to Jerry at IP, ASAP." Even at 5:36 p.m., in May, the sun here is radioactive, magnificent, all-powerful. It pulls at the hearts of people and makes them feel quite alone. This occurs to Zero as he idles in traffic at the unendurable Grant intersection. He'll need to wait at least three lights, he estimates. He longs for a new message from Quiet Woman, he considers calling his wife, he considers calling Alyssa, he considers the poetry of his thoughts. His own secretary is a stuffed old hen—good at what she does, with him five years. He appreciates the invisibility and competence of her work, and he knows himself well enough now to stick with an assistant who leaves him cold. For continuity's sake, one mustn't, in this instance, mix business with pleasure. Still, despite Mrs. Margi Vance's rigid ways and consummate professionalism, despite the fact that she would never second-guess him, Zero doesn't give in to his *most* fanciful asides in these tapes that she will transcribe. He keeps on task: the business of interpreting the world. With his son moved out now and his daughter at her friend's house this week (Luz: friend and nanny—"She'll be having fun, probably forget everything she's learned in school this year," Zero said to Hanna), and with Hanna herself in Phoenix, he's alone. Besides perhaps Maria, the housekeeper, no one will be home when he gets there. This fact intrudes somehow into the controlled climate of the car, a secondary pressure.

Alyssa likes seafood, she told him.

He remembers running after Hanna on the beach in Hawaii, infinite years ago, when she was young (but she lives forever, she must live forever!). She is tall and blond, and at that time she looked like an amazing bird. When he caught up with her, she crumpled, pulling her knees in, her long legs tucked underneath her body, sand on her white shorts, her gorgeous tanned knees. He pushed her back, and in his mind's eye she is smiling, laughing silently behind the mess of her hair, and he ripped the buttons of that silly blouse—not on purpose! But it was so fragile, what was even the point of a shirt like that?—and he pulled down the straps of her bra and settled his own tanned hands inside, his fingers starfish on the white of her breasts, her nipples taut in the tropical evening air. Over the years, he liked to think of her body when she was talking—and talk she did—regaling him with this or that: the new website for her design company, the conference she had with Laurabell's teacher, the antics of her parents, who were always good for a laugh. It helped him smile and enjoy and not care so much about all the time passing. But when she was pouting or snarling at him, which seemed to be half the time now, or when she was simply being businesslike, a partner in this venture—this family, this house and garden, this club, this set of friends, these travel plans, these patterns—then he would forget her body, that dear body underneath the clothing. Oh, how he longed for the body. How the body is truth, at the core.

Doctors! Assholes, most of them. Fucking sons of bitches, pricks, fuckheads—he should know what it is to be an arrogant asshole, plenty enough of them at Raytheon, he's well aware. He knows this part of himself too, sure. It seems to him now—a fleeting thought—that he sent Hanna to Phoenix so he wouldn't have to experience *the room* himself, whatever fucking room the doctor was in, the procedures, the tests, the waiting, the paperwork—it pulls you up short, doesn't it? The frank indignity, the petty bureaucracy of it all. The stupidity of the receptionists, anesthetized themselves—lumps of flesh with dull eyes and limp fingers at their keyboards, losing patient records, mixing up blood samples, sending people to rooms to wait for no reason—a circus of lies and mismanagement. A kangaroo hospital.

"Call Alyssa."

"Calling Alyssa, mobile."

"Hello, Alyssa." Quiet Woman is quiet. The coolness of the leather surrounding Zero's body feels, for a moment, chillier.

"Zero!" she says. She damages him—that's the only way he can describe it. He nestles into this feeling, as sound curls into a seashell.

"Are you busy tonight? I need to see you. I want to take you to dinner."

"But—oh!"

He can hear Hanna turning in the warm air; he can hear the *sluff sluff sluff* of her bare feet padding off, trying to get momentum in the sand. He can see her running again now—but for her it must be some kind of nightmare because she's barely moving at all. Almost a laugh, how easy it will be to catch her. And so he gives her a head start. He is smiling, the wide smile of a handsome man, eyes green as a jaguar's, sultry yet sharp, a shrewd sharpening when he sees something he likes or doesn't like. His nose is what used to be called Roman—and it's sad you don't see that many Roman noses anymore—and his cheekbones are wide and prominent, his jaw set in an impossibly strong manner. Even so, there is a loose confidence to his whole carriage, to the whole grand face and armature. Alyssa knows this. Alyssa has said yes. And so he hangs up, *hanging up* in this case meaning the call just disappears, and Zero is alone again, with Quiet Woman, in the car. "Approaching River Road. Continue straight as Alvernon Way becomes River Road." The solace of the Foothills has begun to permeate that which surrounds him, the visual detritus and stimulus of the valley diminishing now. Hobbies are best when they engage and excite, when they steal attention, eat away the afternoon or evening hours. Hobbies are necessary for a man of responsibility, a man with the lives of so many under his direction. It *is* lonely at the top, let's face it! "If only everyone would do as I say," Zero actually says out loud. Quiet Woman doesn't respond, doesn't deign to say anything until it's time for him to "Stay right," and then "After three hundred feet, turn right onto North Hacienda Del Sol Road."

On cue, he turns. North toward the Catalinas, the ascent.

"Your destination is approaching. . . . After three hundred feet, turn right at 4772 North Hacienda Del Sol Road. . . . You have reached your destination."

Zero climbs the driveway in his car. Hanna herself designed the approach to their home. It was important, she said, to make reference to the region, to invite in the natural beauty of the desert, letting it infuse the ebb and flow of color and texture. Another one of her ideas was that the impact of a home is never stronger than upon first impression. But so few visitors actually do come here. Maria takes the second driveway leading to the back of the property, as does Luz. Zero doesn't notice the saguaros that they purchased, taller than men, or the artificial stream running perpendicular to the driveway, going underground, and then coming back up on the other side, or the solitary hawk sitting on a palo verde to his right, watching the gleaming car as it meanders uphill. He doesn't even notice anymore, not really, the panoramic views, neither the jagged sweep of mountain behind the house, nor, like a skirt falling from the waist of an old-fashioned girl, the city itself, a magic show of twinkling lights at night, reduced to a gray maze in the sun. Zero sits in his car in front of the house. It's as if he knows something is coming, some trepidation, like a sneeze. The wave comes over him hard and fast. He covers his face with his hands and shouts out, one outrageous cry. It's not a command, no one is listening, and then it is over. Zero takes his hands away from his face. What he needs to do: construct a near future. He will make a reservation at Ghost Fish, he'll put a call in to Hanna. Zero gathers his phone, recorder, and keys. His house is a magnificent palace. The hawk is gone.

In Equal Measure

She felt most of all that he was beautiful. In the beginning, she had let herself hope he was in a certain way *for her*, that he'd been sent down to earth as her twin, the finishing of something left undone.

The first time Artesia saw him—blond, radiant—she was making salads in the kitchen at the restaurant. The lettuce came in squat cardboard crates from California, "Bella Fruit & Vegetable" written in old-fashioned script on both the crates and the truck they came in on. The pretty, faded lettering reminded Artesia of movie poverty: boxy cars huffing by, wandering girls in dresses made of chicken-feed sacks. What those girls lacked in funds they made up for in pluck, maybe virtue. At least while the camera was rolling. What would you do today to create that scene—how would you costume the poor? Artesia thought of other girls in her GED class, the one whose blouse was ripped along the shoulder, a little ladder of seeing skin. She thought of the tannish gray people who stand around and have nowhere to go, who never shower. Artesia and her sister and mother have a shower. Of course they have a shower.

Artesia's mother says, *So long as you have a job, you aren't poor.*

Heads of lettuce like fluffy friends, gleaming green under the water. The tomatoes come in a tight plastic bag and the mushrooms are packed into balsa-wood squares. Cucumbers, red cabbage, red onions, heaps of carrots—the raw product seems redundant, extravagant, before she sets to it: cuts, rips, slices. Artesia drowns the lettuce, lets it pop up again. She looks at all the colors.

Her hands were chilly in the sink when he came in with Mario. If she had to put a description to Mario, she'd say he was a scarf of sound, in the air long before he arrived and still unfurling after he was gone. Managers come in their own special boxes, too, like lettuce, like mushrooms. That day, Mario was wearing a steel-gray shirt and silver tie, nightclub worthy. It was almost five when they unlocked the front door. Late May in Tucson, which is like saying that outside is an incinerator.

"This one's fish only, don't even think about putting anything in here. Sacred ground, Ghost Fish Grill—right? Not ghost room, not ghost customer. Here's the walk-in, multiple-use facility. Chef's got his meat and fish in here, his side vegetables, his dairy backup. Bar backup, house wine, beer, the fancy-ass root beer in the bottles, these two shelves. Here you've got your butter patties, your lemons. You'll be cutting up a dozen at least before the shift even begins, sometimes more. Always check how many are left from lunch. You want to get, I don't know, ten slices out of every lemon. Lemons are expensive—you want to know how many waters we serve every night? So you're not going to be hacking the fucking lemons. Beautiful thin slices, nice and attractive. It all adds up. You might not think it matters but it does. This is Artesia, sous chef. What's up, Artesia? This is Paul."

The young man trailing Mario was wearing a skullcap, bright curls emerging from underneath the black wool, around his ears and over his eyes, a fringe of sunlight or gold. He was tall but not gawky, thin, not fragile. Jeans, a black T-shirt.

"What's up," said Artesia.

"What's up," said Paul.

"She gets the salads ready, salads and vegetables and bread, right, Artesia? Servers dress the salads, put butter bowls in with the bread. You've got your bleu cheese, your ranch, your vinaigrette, your fucking *diet* raspberry vinaigrette. What's this—what is this?"

"Plain oil and vinegar."

"Some people want it on the side. Yes sir, yes ma'am. On the side, here you go—little bowls just for you. Your word is precious. Your word, your desires, whatever you want. The tub is always filled with ice—beyond important to keep the dressings cold, we don't want anybody getting salmonella and suing our asses, then we're all out of a job, see what I mean? Dishwasher station, pretty obvious. Bus it in, separate out the knives, blade the fuck down, glasses, napkins in here . . ."

They shared a look underneath the Mario sound scarf. Paul's eyes—they were filled with light. They seemed to shed light—actual illumination—in the poorly configured kitchen, with the anti-light fluorescents and the stainless steel and grease-stained walls, with no windows at all except one peeking window in the back door.

What is beauty? Its personal nature was what Artesia felt at that moment. Not just discrimination, but exclusion. Everyone excluded but her.

They were hammered that night. Maybe two dozen, four dozen times Paul came running in with his tray and his blond hair (skullcap disappeared) and his flitting light-shine eyes, and then he was gone again. They didn't speak much except for the rudiments. *Here you go, these are fresh. Here's a new bleu. Thanks much. Party of eight just sat down, lettuce eaters all of them.* He wore a green shirt like all the busboys, which seemed obscurely absurd.

At ten, Artesia arranged one last overcooked broccoli stalk in a sad curl and put up three salads. She swabbed the sink, took out the trash, restocked bowls and forks and dressing tubs, checked inventory, made a note to get more onions. After clocking out, she stood for a moment by the coffeemaker. He was talking to a four-top: two men wearing summer shirts and their dates, probably wives, lithe and soft-focus. All four watched Paul, recognition in their faces, as if he were telling them a story, revealing who he was, who they were.

Artesia turned and walked back through the kitchen, said *later* to the chef and weird Richard. Staff parked out back, by the Dumpsters. She kicked one of the cardboard boxes that had fallen close to her car. They were like movie-set blocks, easy to knock over. Her car started— *woo-hoo!* Always a moment of relief. Then there was the regular clatter of hard-to-interpret sounds as she backed out, accelerated past the Lexuses and Hondas and BMWs in front of Ghost Fish, and drove out onto the street. A second set of unusual sounds occurred as she coasted downhill, back into glittering glimmering chameleon Tucson.

Her mother was out with asshole-of-the-year Rudy, and her sister—little Chelsea, technically her stepsister—was at a sleepover, so their apartment in Oasis Palms was her own that night, for what it was worth. She drank some flat Diet Coke, took a shower. At one, Artesia was lying on top of her sheets, in the prism created by the lights on Alvernon and from the courtyard. (The pool on the courtyard's far side was drained, as it had been all ten months they'd lived here.) The objects in her room looked unreal. The standard late-night vacuuming, bat hunting, recitations, and strenuous sex in 2B had simmered down, and the traffic sounded like waves, an uneven and yet still relaxing metronome.

Paul. Paul Coleridge. She'd looked at his time card.

It really did seem true that every single person was different and every single person had something wonderful and unique about him, or her. You never knew what would happen next. There were surprises in the world, like marbles scattered on the desert floor.

Their shifts lined up on Thursday and Friday nights and on Wednesdays, lunch. The next Friday, Paul came out back with Nico and Artesia to get stoned. They stood behind the Dumpsters, heads bowed. If you looked from a distance, all you could see was black hair, black hair, blond hair. Three in prayer.

Nico always talked super slow, so you had to be patient with him. He'd started working at Ghost Fish a couple of months ago. Maybe something was going on with his papers, he was a little squirrelly about that, although this didn't stop him from—maybe it helped spur him on in—inviting Artesia to smoke some really fairly damn decent weed before or after their shift, and sometimes on a slow night, midshift too. Nico was twenty-five, maybe thirty, with a head of wispy curls like a toddler's. His eyes were half-closed, entreating. He had no tattoos on his skinny arms, but he had a hatching of cuts and scars. He could wash dishes like a motherfucker.

The space between the Dumpsters and the concrete wall smelled like piss and garbage, but on some days Artesia thought it wasn't so much piss as greasewood or coffee grounds. It was worse after rain, which hadn't occurred in, oh, a billion years.

Paul said, "That's the way my cat is, too," when Artesia said that her cat sometimes stared at her like she was Satan. Just like out of the blue.

"Yeah, you have a cat?"

The two of them were futzing around in the dirt with their feet, a red high top with a white toe shadowed with words and pictures (Artesia's), and a Vans sneaker in suave suede (Paul's). They were using their feet to line up little stones, then knock them toward the other person. Nico was rolling a second joint.

"Miss Gray, I call her. She was just hanging around my house when I moved in, sitting on the patio all heartbroken. So I fed her this can of tuna I had. Now she's in love." Here came a smile, with tiny golden wrinkles around his eyes and everything.

"A stray? My mom would kill me if I brought a stray in."

"She's no stray. She's a traveler."

"Cats stink," said Nico. "They stink up."

Neither of the others was listening to him. The sky was filled with birdsong, a net of gauzy gold thread.

"Meow," Paul Coleridge said.

"Meow," Artesia said back.

Normal weekend craziness that night, but then management had to throw in a Memorial Day two-for-one margarita and mojito special, too. By eight, Artesia had prepped a third tub of lettuce, and Jax, the even-on-a-regular-night lunatic chef, had thrown a knife (it was a small knife), which lodged in the wall two feet from the food prep sink, because the broiler flame kept going out.

The dishes were washed, though—washed and gleaming. Nico's head bent to the job, no problem. And no real problems for Artesia either, knife notwithstanding. It was busy, but so what? Paul and Les (the other busboy) and the three servers kept running in and out of the kitchen. Every few minutes there he was, smiling.

At a break she stood by the coffeemaker, drinking a Sprite. A whole passel of rich people chomped on their salads and picked bones from rare-species fish (they paid extra to get the fish whole, as in straight out of the stream, and then they set to their ineffectual disemboweling). There was a man who looked like some kind of movie director, a white guy as brown-skinned as Nico, tan from a booth or a can, and a younger woman with gleaming hair, as if she spent a lifetime brushing it every morning. Sometimes Artesia felt they were duping the customers, with the thirty-dollar entrées and nine-dollar "handcrafted" pralines. If she had thirty dollars, she'd buy a sandwich and pocket the other twenty-five. There was Paul, taking the rich director dude's glass and filling it with water. Giving him the smile, too. She could see the shape of his shoulders from here.

Mario came barreling over so she retreated, her hands in the lettuce tub by the time he got to the kitchen. Nico was eating a chunk of salmon left on a plate. He dumped it when Mario appeared.

Five minutes later, Paul came in. He cupped his hand for a split second around her waist and whispered, "Here's trouble. They let out the salad lady. Run for the hills, gentlemen!" Her face burned when he said this, and she looked down, plunging her hands still farther into the cold water where she was rinsing radishes. He was gone again.

At the end of the night she looked for him, but he had already left. He'd punched out. It was only Mario and Jax at the bar.

"Meow," she whispered to herself, in the car on the way back down the hill.

Artesia's mother was sitting in the living room when Artesia got home. Artesia could sketch out her mother's evening: Smirnoff Ice (raspberry) or Mike's Hard Lemonade. *American Idol, CSI: Miami, Criminal Minds,* and, finally, anything at all. Some '80s movie was on now. *Top Gun?* Stories went through Monica's head parallel to the TV shows, stories featuring a girl gone wild. Artesia kept breaking molds. She'd broken the baby mold, she'd broken the soft-girl-in-her-mother's-arms mold, she'd broken the gangly girl-power mold, and now she was, Monica had made clear, a stranger in Monica's home.

"And where has *she* been this evening?" said Monica, from the shadows of the room. Sitting square and still, as if she herself was a chair.

"What? I was at work. And hi to you too, Mom."

"Work? Right, they're still serving at midnight. You're fucking with me, Artesia."

My name is Monica, and I have been married twice. I live in Tucson and work in the retail business. I enjoy watching TV, relaxing, shopping, going to the movies, and spending time with family.

"What are you talking about?" It was going to be one of the bad nights, Artesia could tell, a different flavor of unpleasant than when Rudy was around.

Yes, Monica had been counting the hours, and now, although she had to know it made everything worse, the weight of her vigilance came crashing down, and there was nowhere to go but out. Words came to her that she didn't even know she had. They were really beautiful, like opalescent stones.

"Where's Chelsea?" asked Artesia, into the splintering fog. "Is Chelsea home?"

"I want to become an artist," said Paul, "to study how the human body is formed, and to express what I see on canvas. That's it. That's my dream."

"Wow," said Artesia. They were sitting on the stoop outside the restaurant, lunch shift over. "Art is cool." She took a last drag of the cigarette and sent it flinging out into the parking lot. Almost hitting Mario's car.

"My parents made me get a job to help pay for summer school. I'm doubling up now so I can take extra studio courses in the fall. They say I've got to contribute. Okay, I understand that."

He looked at her. His eyes looked all over her, as if he were studying the human form now.

"I have to help with the rent because my mom's job pays like crap, and I don't want to have to move and have Chelsea change schools again. Chelsea's my little sister. Did I tell you about her?"

"Yeah, you did. And have I mentioned that you are—you're like my hero, Artesia."

"Yeah, right!"

One last hobbling rich person came out of the restaurant to make his way to his car—no, make that two—a wife was tottering out of the building also, pulling up the rear. The weather on this particular day was perfect, divine; they were in heaven. The Catalinas stretching out behind the restaurant were bleached out and soft, as if they'd been dusted with sugar.

Artesia simmered in the beauty of it all for a moment, and then she turned to Paul and said, because it seemed like the right thing to say on this afternoon of bliss: "You're *my* hero, Paul."

He was still smiling when she said it, smiling into the sun behind her, but two things happened at once. His smile remained a fraction too long, as a smile does when you're posing for the camera. And Artesia's words sounded different than his. Her words did not sound like banter.

It had seemed that there was beauty and intelligence in the world, yes. It had seemed there was a person to take this ride with, and that you, too, had something to offer.

Every night yielded a surprise at home, although then, too, there was repetition, or a kind of trammeling tradition. Artesia always looked in on Chelsea, who was short for her age and had a slight speech impediment, and at night had a funny habit of sleeping while kind of kneeling, leaning over her bent knees into the pillow, her face smashed into Cinderella's skirt or Nemo's smile. After work, Artesia went into the bedroom and gently knocked her sister over. She pulled the blanket out from under a heavy leg and tucked it up near the girl's chin.

Her mother was in the bedroom, crying or talking on the phone or both—it was hard to tell what was going on in there. Artesia let her be. She knew things were hard for her mother.

She brought the plastic liter bottle half filled with a filched batch of margarita mix and tequila down to the courtyard. Lights were on in some apartments, but smashed curtains and broken blinds prevented any of the residents from seeing out, seeing her. Artesia opened the creaking chain link gate and walked up to the edge of the empty pool. The moon was high above Oasis Palms. She walked down two concrete steps and sat on the third, where the water would have lapped right over her, had there been water.

They'd only had sex once before he disappeared. He followed her down the hill one night after work because he thought it was crazy that people partied in an empty swimming pool, and he had to see it for himself. They'd already had a couple of drinks in her car and shared a last joint with Nico, until he waved behind his back and disappeared into a rusted-out sedan driven by an older man, tiny behind the wheel. They were laughing. "So your life is like a barrel of fun, huh? Vast concrete holes appeal?" Paul said, and she shoved him, and then he said, "I want to see your kitty, too. See if she thinks I'm the devil, like you are." Artesia and Paul. Paul and Artesia. Don't let anyone tell you that you can't fall in love in just minutes, or a few restaurant hours. Nor is there ever, or has there ever been, any *why*—except the complete why and wherefore, the DNA structure, the uncompromised everything. It was as if it had already happened, and you can't go back in time without something really fucked up happening.

Chelsea shouted and came running when they opened the door. Artesia hugged the girl and told her she should be asleep, this was ridiculous, all kung fu princesses were in bed by now. When they went into the living room, Artesia was glad to see her mother was not drunk, that she was in good order. "You should have told me you had someone coming over," Monica said, then, "Hello," in a shy voice, younger than a mother's. Paul leaned over the cocktail table to shake her hand. He wasn't wearing a suit—he was still wearing a bright green work shirt—but he looked like a gentleman at that moment. He was acting like a gentleman. All that can potentially occur with gentlemen passed before the eyes of all concerned, then Monica sat back down in front of the television as if he weren't even there. Good, said part of Artesia to the other part of Artesia. The sound of the TV was like the noise at the restaurant, an eternal din. Chelsea had folded herself over the top of the recliner. She was rocking the chair by making contact with one bare foot on the carpet and pushing off. The clustering of responsibility: this was what Artesia wished away when she was wishing at all. "C'mon," she said, pulling Paul to the kitchen.

Paul stood with his hands in his pockets, looking for Snickers the devil-sniffing cat, maybe, though he didn't say anything about that now. He just stood there in his black cap with his brilliant golden hair and his jeans and his sneakers while she got two coffee mugs and set them on the counter, and then pulled out an ice tray and started twisting it and extracting cubes and filling the mugs with as much ice as she could get, which didn't turn out to be more than slivers, broken off from some fault of the brittle white trays it wouldn't come out of. He was impatient, she thought, sorrowful and out of place. She hurried, smashing the ice tray on the counter.

"Artesia, Artesia, aren't you going to tell me a story?" called Chelsea, as Artesia and Paul went out the door.

It was bright outside, the moon and then the prison-style spotlight hitting the center of the courtyard. They walked through the glare to the empty pool, stepping down into the shallow end. It was calmer, darker here. Artesia played hostess, arranging the two lawn chairs, putting the mugs on a sun-shredded table. Paul poured the drinks. "This is the fucking life," he said, surveying the three walls of the buildings surrounding them, the chipped paint of the pool. He walked her into the deep end and pushed her against the pale blue of yesterday. "I'm going to drown you now," he whispered. "We're going to drown together." That was the first time they kissed. Pretty soon they were running and veering, shouting and whispering, out the gate of the courtyard and into the parking lot. They got in his car and drove halfway down the alley, nestling in near a Dumpster.

It was more mortal than she expected, but there were moments of transcendence when she forgot herself, when she radiated in an almost shameful way, as if what they were doing were taboo, something that should not, should never happen—at the same time that it was the most right thing in the world.

He worked three more shifts at the restaurant, and then her twin was gone. Art classes started? College fund all set now? He had stopped answering his phone.

An Island of Animals

His main idea was that this would be the night. He'd been dating Sarah, in his manner, for a couple of months. Not clear if it was working. Seemed possible it was not. And yet she was so nice. So tonight he would decide once and for all, and be done with the searching conversations and all the other searching for this and that.

At seven, Wilbur pulled up in front of 1293 Felicitas los Coyotes, stucco already cracking on this and many identical buildings in Sunset los Coyotes, a "community" you couldn't exactly call gated because there was no gate, though there had been, the whole time he'd been coming here, the lonely posts for such a gate, and an intercom box with no innards. It was a new street and a new world, and apparently the street makers had a yen for regionalism, if no particular knowledge of Spanish. (Still, the luckyish coyotes were probably a less painful invocation than a "Constitution Street" or a "Village Garden Avenue," gruesome assertions of the kind of civilization found on the other side of the continent.) He took a gander at his phone before he went in—a compulsion, of course, Wilbur wouldn't deny it—and saw that he had no new messages, neither texts nor e-mails nor voice mails, and though he had a quick, burning desire to check ESPN, he finally decided to put the phone down—*Put the phone down, Wilbur! Back away from the ledge!*—and walk up the path to Sarah's abode.

He was dimly aware of the plantings on either side of the blanched red stepping-stones, plunged into the deathlike soil of the desert. At worst, the soil wasn't soil at all but caliche, a mineral fusion created by calcium carbonate binding together all the ordinary gravel and clay and sand into an inhospitable rocklike layer, whereas in a sweet land there might be soft, delicious earth. Sarah found pleasure in her gardening, though she also complained *unceasingly* about the conditions here, Wilbur found, and found hard to understand. You should enjoy yourself. And he meant this in *any* sense. He could understand the pleasures, for instance, of productivity, of bettering oneself. It wasn't all just margaritas at dawn and cockfights behind the Target on Broadway. But still, why do something if you were just going to *fucking complain about it afterward?*

The plants most recently planted by Sarah were a few thrumming cacti—the fluffed out fireworks kind—and then some flowers in red, pink, and white. The better part of the yard was covered in pale pink gravel of a variety popular throughout Sunset los Coyotes. The plants, however, were virtually invisible to Wilbur (let alone their proper names). He had commented on them last week, at her behest, and now he was done. Plants were plants. Yard work, landscaping—he cared not about that.

He rang the bell and Sarah opened the door.

"Hey," said Wilbur.

"Hey," said Sarah, with a smile. "Let me just feed Lala, and then I'll be ready. Come on in, baby."

In the foyer, she reached out her arms for him and rose up on her toes for a kiss.

This was what Sarah looked like: Sarah was tall (but he was taller). She had played volleyball in college; he'd seen the pictures of her on court. There she was next to the other rangy girls and the suited men. His giraffe. His Sarah. These days she often wore tops that revealed her arms, which were long and graceful and seemed always to be doing something gentle or helping. Helping by picking up a dime that fell in the parking lot, for instance. Helping him tuck in his shirt just a little bit more in the back. Helping put the dishes away, stacking them in a rinsed cluster before placing them in the dishwasher. Yes, her arms were long, and in their first embraces, it thrilled him—how very long and far away she could reach. How when they were kissing, there was just no stopping her. Not only could she handily cup his balls or lay confident pressure on the shaft of his penis, but suddenly there her hand was, down still farther, behind him, seeking out his anus, finding his anus—as if he were in bed with Reed Richards!

She was "feisty." Actually, he wasn't so sure she *was* feisty, but that was how one interpreted the look of Sarah. She often wore her wavy blond hair in a ponytail high on her head, and she had three silver hoops in one ear, one hoop in the other. This was a throwback to the college girl of days gone by, because now Sarah was a responsible citizen overall, a vice assistant (or something like that) at the University of Arizona.

They spoke, at times, of her job.

Wilbur himself was an IT guy—high-end IT. Meaning he was actually designing software for a small, ruthless company run by a Norwegian. Norwegians, Wilbur had found, were notorious criminals. But it was all right to be criminal *for the right reasons.* There was a kind of criminality that was really not criminal. "Criminal" implies "caught." They were not *caught*—neither Wilbur nor Dagfinn.

Dagfinn: he was really a piece of work. The company made millions. Dagfinn himself had only come to this damn country ten years ago. He was like the American Dream *ripped*, he was a stud, a weird Norwegian stud. The man actually looked like nothing, like a dweeb—Wilbur was not vain, but he *knew* he was better looking than that Norwegian freakazoid millionaire—and yet people just kept shoveling money at him. And girls. And wives. Dagfinn had had plenty—both, every, simultaneous, serial. But Wilbur, too, was an integral part of the team now. With Dagfinn, his dark-knight cousin Gunnar, two other longtime Norwegian suck-up associates, and then Ann in Marketing, who may as well have been a man, for all anyone thought of her.

"Hey, I forgot to tell you," Sarah said, throwing her tall, blond, ponytailed, long-armed self over to the other side of the kitchen. She handed him a coupon. "Look—pretty good deal, right?"

Wilbur looked down at what was in his hand. "Yeah."

"I love that place anyway—should we go?"

"Sure, if that's what you feel like. I haven't had Greek in a while."

She came back around to his side of the quartzite pony bar. "Twenty-five bucks each, with a bottle of wine," she cleared up for him, in case he couldn't read.

"Yeah, I like it." He felt like he was repeating himself now.

On the counter, Lala the gray cat was either hacking up her food or chewing it into smaller bits to eat later. Wilbur had no idea why Sarah fed Lala on the counter. There was no dog here. There were no small children. The place was sterile of all life except for Lala and Sarah.

"Oh shoot," Sarah said, hurrying toward the paper towels.

"What do the Greeks eat, anyway? Ambrosia?" asked Wilbur, driving.

Sarah was looking wistfully out onto Tanque Verde. There was a man in a dinosaur suit in front of a tire store. He was waving a sign with large orange letters. Wilbur was Sarah's first boyfriend in a year, she'd told him. She'd been celibate for a *year.*

"Ambrosia, yes." She turned to Wilbur with a smile. "Although I'll probably have something that comes with Greek salad. I love Greek salad. And there's stuffed grape leaves, spanakopita, moussaka—God, I love moussaka—yummy lamb, all kinds of stuff like that, everything just *dripping* with olive oil."

Sarah turned back toward the view. When you're on Tanque Verde closing in on central Tucson, there's actually nothing to wistfully stare at but for men in dinosaur suits, the twenty-foot T. rex in front of McDonald's, and a few crappy pieces of wood furniture splintering in the late afternoon sun outside secondhand stores. (For those who haven't been to Tucson, who don't know the situation with the heat, we'll offer this: Living here is like being sent up in a space capsule too close to the sun, or flying like Icarus right into the jagged rays of the sun, then shaken until you're brain-dead as an old egg. Being here, in Tucson, the sun is commander—if you can picture that. The sun is everywhere, in every nook and cranny, and there is no nook or cranny left cool or dim. A person could go mad in this heat. Zero nuance. There is crawling indoors for some relief, and there is standing in the force field, and there is no in-between. Night is just a giving-up at the end of the day, an exhausted turning away, before the next day begins.)

Wilbur felt a pang of anxiety, which he took as a need to check his phone.

At the restaurant, she spoke quietly and forcefully about something meaningful to her. The restaurant was a bit like a cave, green plastic plant-forms hanging inside coves and a large fresco depicting a grandmotherly sort walking up a path and holding an urn. In a smaller fresco on the opposite wall, you could "look into" a window and see a family eating a meal—their foodstuffs including small black circles and swirls of red and brown and green. The frescoes were extremely, *extremely* primitive, which put Wilbur on edge.

The meaningful thing was a paper she was writing for a conference on distance learning.

" . . . and after that draft, I said to myself, I don't know if I can even *do* this. This is what I've spent my life doing—all my education, all my experience in the field—and then here I go again, I'm in front of the computer, and my brain goes *whoosh!*—out the window like a damn . . ." She gestured something indistinct.

"Like a fly? A bird?"

"Sometimes I wonder if maybe I should be doing something else. Thirty-two isn't completely over the hill, right? I could be anything, really. I could do anything. I could be a vet if I wanted to."

"Yeah, you'd have to have gone into the military."

"No, silly—I mean a *veterinarian*. Bowwow, woof woof? Animals. I love animals. I could be doing that. When I think about how much I love little Lala, for instance. Or the abandoned dogs and cats, they are in such need. Oh, I can hardly stand it sometimes!"

"Lala, yes. But Sarah, that's a good question—let me ask you." Wilbur leaned back a bit in the wrought-iron chair (the entire decorating scheme was "garden" here). His beer rested on the table before him. Sarah was drinking Greek sangria, white wine based, with melon and oranges. "Let's just say you've got one life to lead, right? Close enough to the truth, yes? What would you say you're missing out on right now? What would you really do to change your life?"

Tall Sarah, who had been hovering somewhat over her wineglass, like some kind of humble nymph looking into a pond, now ever so slightly shrunk back in her chair, a tiny pink smirch on each cheek. "What would I do to change it? You mean, like becoming a veterinarian?"

"Yes, is that what it really is? Is that what you're missing out on?"

He was sure there was something to ferret out, and he was willing—eager—to listen, even if it were awkward. The semi-embarrassed, semi-bold expression illuminating her face was familiar to him, not so much from conversations, but from more physical moments, when *yak yak yak* wasn't so important. It was the look she got in bed when she was preparing to make one of her more supposedly adventurous sexual advances.

"Oh—"

"Take me," Wilbur said, shrugging. "For me, what I've got is I'm missing the opportunity to be noticed by the right people. At TDS, we're going places, *I'm* going places. But the fact is, I could jump right over Dagfinn and Gunnar if I was in the right location. L.A., New York. I'm missing the opportunity to be in the company of my peers. I know that sounds arrogant, but what I'm saying is, someday I'll *see* my chance—and because I've identified it already, I'll take it. I'll step into this place I've created in my imagination. So that's me. Now come on, your turn."

She smiled faintly. She hesitated, and then in her quiet voice said, "I feel that I'm missing . . . a real relationship with another person. Not that you and I don't have a real relationship right now—we do, Wilbur. But I mean, what I hope to do, what I mean is—" Here Sarah looked back up from the melon pond. "I'd like a deeper relationship. Someday, when the time is right, of course. Like you're saying—just imagining—so when it comes, I'll see it. I'll be—I think I'm ready for that."

She looked pretty in the yellow sweater that she had put on to shield herself from the air-conditioning chill here in the bullshit Greek garden. She *was* pretty, anyway. She had good breasts, with wide, soft areolas and little teeny tiny nipples. She was two years younger than he was, which didn't matter that much right now, but as she got older—well, actually, it really didn't seem to matter.

"Ah, the future," he said philosophically. He felt it was important to keep her comfortable, in any case. As a surgeon would, any good doctor. "I get it. I see. So, how's that Greek sangria, anyway? I never knew there was such a thing."

"*Mmm*, yum. Do you want a sip?"

"Oh, no, no. All right—I'll take a sip, sure, why not?" Wilbur leaned across the table and picked up the wineglass. He rotated the lemon slice away from his mouth and drank.

"Great. Tangy."

"Isn't it?"

She seemed to have an anxious, questioning way of being right then, and he knew he would have to pump up the jocular. But before he worked that particular angle, the server appeared to take their dinner order. He was a surly, pimply boy—probably some kind of Greek, thought Wilbur, rather tired overall of immigrants (the Norwegians), and never having really liked Greek food.

"So one of these meat dishes. Lamb. Can you recommend one? I like barbecue. A good steak, that type of deal. Do you have a barbecued lamb tonight?"

The teenager looked at him in a not-seeing-him fashion he'd probably perfected with his prick Greek parents. He deadpanned, "We have the marinated lamb, the lamb shanks, the dolma, the gyros. We've got all kinds of lamb." At the end of this announcement, the teen looked away, toward the grandmother walking up the path with her peg legs in the fresco. He waited, holding his pad.

Wilbur pursed his lips ostentatiously, not willing to be hurried. "You've got French fries, right? As a side?"

"Sure."

"All right, I tell you what. I'll have the lamb shanks—lamb shanks, and a side of fries. That'll be great."

Sarah ordered the moussaka, as well as her side salad. She suggested a salad for him too, and to be amiable, he got one. He also had a passing thought, which was that he hadn't known she'd ever wanted to be a veterinarian. It's funny the things you find out about a person. *Animals*—just the word made him flinch. It had all started when his mother named him after that pig. What a fucking stupid idea.

The salads came, topped with onion slices. She began ferrying hers over to the side plate—and, even now the possible lover, he did it with his as well. For a moment, he had a sad thought about not being able to have sex tonight, if things didn't go right, if the answers didn't stack up to her advantage. Not that he'd made up his mind yet. She could still be alive in all this. The game wasn't over.

They talked about work for a while, a little cooling off period for both of them: Wilbur from inquest and Sarah from revelation. She asked how the project was going.

"No change. It's out of our hands now. I'd say this guy the big D hired is going to crush the living souls out of them."

She smiled, her eyes gleaming with something like admiration. He ate another mouthful of salad and then pushed his plate to the side.

The rebel-wannabe teenager took away their salads and came back with the entrées. Sarah started talking about the conference again, and a planning meeting she and her boss had this week with some academic types. The conversation reminded Wilbur of what it must be like to be married, what married people did together. Over Monday's meatloaf or Tuesday's leftovers, a kind of download of what happened during the hours, days, weeks, years.

Sarah methodically ate her four-by-four slab of moussaka. She cut a square of eggplant and piled the sauce and meat on top, and then carried the whole small freight from the plate to her mouth. She did this two dozen times, each time exactly the same set of movements as the last. They had met through an online dating service. She'd listed her interests as "good food, good wine, good conversation" and her looks as "pretty, long blond hair, athletic build," and her picture more or less corroborated that. She was on the beach in the photograph, leaning back and smiling at the camera. You could see waves and colorful blurs of people behind her. She wore a bikini top and athletic shorts. It had been the second time Wilbur used the service. The first go-around, he'd dated the girl a few times—and then she dumped *his* ass. It was during the intervening months that Wilbur had said to himself, really said to himself, that he wanted to get married, he wanted to settle down, he wanted to be in a real relationship. The whys and wherefores remained indistinct, and yet it was a keen desire—and a natural one. Who didn't want to get married? That's what you did. Look at Dagfinn and his wife. The wife was always hustling to and from La Encantada or the Foothills Mall, returning Brooks Brothers shirts, buying birthday presents, picking up lobsters for dinner. He was too old now to hang out with Justin and Joe, his beer-and-burger partners—shit, they weren't really going *anywhere*.

And yet you needed to find the right woman. The right woman was out there.

"All right, I've got another question for you," he said. The lamb had too much cinnamon on it. Cinnamon—what the fuck? The girl who broke up with him was a brunette. Petite. Sexy. Good dresser. She worked at Raytheon.

"You're interesting tonight, with all your questions. Okay, what next?"

Sarah was trying to sound relaxed, but there was a touch of worry in her voice. If he did still want to follow through—if he wanted to carry on with this, with her—he was going to have to go the extra mile in terms of getting back to that psychological spot where they'd go ahead and have sex tonight, back at her place, with Lala the ceaselessly shedding angora, Sarah's hair and the silky cat hair both catching in his throat, all over her bed, on her pillows.

"What's your fatal flaw? I know, I know, weird question. Everyone's got one though, so what's yours?"

"My fatal flaw?"

"Yup. And then I'll tell you mine." His phone was buzzing in his pants.

He thought she might say something about working too hard—this was a little theme in her life already, he'd noticed. Or maybe something about being so focused on the details, the small things, that she forgot the important stuff, so that she'd basically be relegated to piss-crap jobs all her life, even if they did keep changing titles. Or maybe something to do with the cat, he wasn't sure what, but it did seem like a flaw, the fucking cat, though he wasn't going to say that—he wasn't going to put words in her mouth. All right, it was this: she funneled all her energy into a scrawny, shedding, ten-pound, throwing-up cat, *a cat*. Or then there was the absurd desert gardening motif. And she talked about painting sometimes; she was the quintessential Sunday painter, or worse, she only *talked* about being a Sunday painter—she was going to have nothing at the end, nothing. She would squander it all. Squandering, that would be her fatal flaw. Not getting it at all, moving too slow.

Sarah's eyes were shining. She spoke softly, almost whispering. "Loving blindly, I think. I don't love more than other people, or better, I'm not saying that, but that I sometimes just—I sometimes just go where my heart is leading me."

"Ah," he said. The second sangria must have gone to her head. At the same time, he could see an etching of consternation on her face, especially her eyebrows.

Anyway, Wilbur found her answer acutely and unnaturally depressing. And, yes, it was a deal breaker for him. He saw clearly the hoop he'd have to jump through—the vulnerable/yucky/relationship hoop—before he could even get *close* to what he was after, the right woman, marriage. The Goal.

He sat upright in his chair. Voilà. Presto. Sarah wasn't a giraffe—she was a dodo bird. Grayish feathers, with a large, soft middle, skin wrapped around the bones like burlap around cement and plaster. Her colorless eyes stared out at him. They had no irises, just squinty black. Her legs were firm; he knew that without even looking under the table. Steely kneecaps and rebar calves and flat, immense feet, and then of course the two puny wings, one on each side, and the thready tail feathers.

It would be immensely easy to leave her.

Wilbur said no to coffee, rubbing his stomach and giving Sarah what he imagined to be a gentle smile. After paying the check, he said in a low voice that he felt a little tired that evening, and so he wouldn't be coming back to her place after all.

He dropped her off, watching as she, knowing but not knowing—he'd text her the skinny later—tiptoed down the path to her condo, the squalid gravel planted with little hopeful clumps and clusters. Wilbur backed up, turned around, and slowly motored toward the main road. His phone was still. The stars had come out, but he couldn't see them with the headlights on. If he had stayed, he and Sarah could have turned off all the lights in the house and on the porch, and they could have frolicked in her desert yard—and beyond. They could have skipped and jumped in the dark, under the summer constellations, some of which he could name— he remembers that he knows their names, from some past life, some past small foray into a good thing.

A Sense of Belonging Burrowing into a Sense of Shame

The sorority girl showed up at the political candidate's headquarters ahead of schedule. The shift didn't start until seven, but she'd given herself more time than she needed to find parking—she was able to park her pale green Bug in the half-empty lot just outside the front door.

It was a low-lying, unostentatious wreck of a building, the besieged adobe brick of territorial Arizona, slim spying windows cut into the corners. She was rarely in this part of town, the edge of South Tucson—a city within the city, very poor—and within spitting distance of the hip, if not a bit too raw, downtown bars. The fleeting bad feelings Marissa had as she approached the building were *will they see my car?* and *my father*.

But no one was paying attention to her, after all. Only one person was in the front room when she walked in—a tall, wispy-bearded guy standing behind a table spread with pamphlets and clipboards. He was staring at his phone. A plastic fishbowl sat in the middle of the table, sample pins wedged on the rim: *Democracy Is Alive!* and *Grijalva!* Some presidential pins had to be in there, too—the somewhat desperate now, getting-more-feverish hope for an ouster.

"Excuse me?" Marissa said. "I'm here to volunteer? I read it online, that you need volunteers?"

The guy looked up. "Yeah, yeah. Definitely," he said, glancing right and left, then patting his chest as if he might have taped pens or directions to his shirt. "Be right back." He skirted the edge of the table and veered past her, disappearing into what looked like a storage room, perhaps, or an inner sanctum, where a few older people—activists—were talking among themselves. Private activist matters.

Marissa Pratt, a sophomore at the University of Arizona and a Chi Chi for almost a year now, felt unfortunately tall herself, as if her head might hit the ceiling à la Alice in Wonderland and the "Drink Me" debacle. She briefly agonized that her brown velour pants with pink satin stripes deflected from her seriousness of intent, were likely to be underappreciated here. But what did it matter what she wore? She'd come to make phone calls.

An older woman with a long gray braid emerged from the Activist Room, followed by the red-shirted guy, now talking on his phone. "You're here to volunteer?" the woman said briskly, not particularly low-key sounding—not liberal in the liberal sense of the word. "Do we have your name and contact information? We need that first. Here, fill this out. And you'll be making calls, I presume? That's *wunderbar*. These are the easy ones—we'll go easy on you. First time, right? These people are all registered, party line, no wolverines in the bunch. We're getting out the vote. Never too early to start. Here's the script. And you're gathering volunteers."

"Volunteers for what?" asked Marissa, trying to keep up and figure out the questions she should get answered right away, such as where exactly would she sit, and what phone would she use.

"Making calls, canvassing—we've got plenty to do here," said the spindly lady, giving her an empty, obliterating smile. A woman Marissa's age with a ponytail and a headset appeared, holding a piece of paper. She and the older woman started speaking in Spanish, leaving Marissa with her clipboard and her own phone and a ball-point pen from Marriott Courtyard.

By quitting time an hour and a half later (*No calls after 8:30 p.m.!* was highlighted in yellow, just under *Be Forceful but Friendly!* and *Get a Commitment!*), Marissa had made thirty-five calls. She had spoken to eight actual people. Mostly she'd read a script into the vacuum of voice mail. She had tried various elocution techniques, settling on a sprightly but intelligent tone she associated with schoolteachers. There was something unbearably awkward about calling people you didn't know, trying to persuade them to do something out of the blue. The first woman she spoke to laughed heartily after she made her pitch. She'd already received three calls from other volunteers.

Five voice mails in, Marissa got a man who seemed to be having difficulty breathing and/or understanding. He asked her to repeat everything she said. He breathed, and thought, and then he took down the information for Saturday's rally. If his daughter could drive him, he'd be there. He said, "May I ask, are you in college? Do you volunteer often?" It appeared he had a lot of time on his hands.

"Sure, sometimes. But anyway, I'm glad you can come on Saturday, maybe. And—and—Mr. Crowler, can we rely on you for just one more thing? Can we rely on you for a donation?"

Mr. Crowler was willing to discuss the ins and outs of his finances, but he couldn't be relied on for a donation, it turned out. Nor was she able to exact donations from any of the other seven people she spoke to, though two did say they'd try to make it on Saturday, one sounding like she meant it. She said she'd already lined up a baby-sitter, and that she knew the address. A couple of others said to call back in the fall.

Marissa filled the bottom half of the sheet, then flipped it over and filled the entire back, marking calls made and the results, her loose, loopy penmanship barely staying in the claustrophobic lines (though still more legible than the jagged scrawl of the previous volunteer). Was this the way it felt to be part of a new ethos, to be caught up in the winds of change? Marissa thought it probably was, and that this was necessary, doing mundane work behind the scenes. She had never tried to make things happen—nationally!—before, and the sense of herself as part of something larger kept her, or *almost* kept her, from feeling too embarrassed making the calls.

At the end of the *H*'s, she stood, tall and awkward again.

Things had heated up in the low-ceilinged building during the last hour. Someone had brought in a couple of pizzas, and a few people, including kids, were eating and watching C-SPAN in a back room. Marissa couldn't find the woman with the braid, so she walked up to the folks stuffing envelopes in the room adjacent to the one with the TV. The only thing besides tables and folding chairs in the room were boxes lined up along one wall. "Do you guys need any help? I was making calls, but it's too late now." She smiled wanly, her adherence to the rules scant membership here. She rubbed the strap of her neon green messenger bag, which she'd brought in because it had her laptop in it, along with some UA notebooks and folders. Her brother had given her the messenger bag for her birthday. It matched her car.

"We need all the help we can get, don't we, Sheila?" said the man with a thick white mustache and a Diamondbacks cap to a squat, sixtyish woman in full denim (shirt, pants, sequined vest and visor). She fluffed a wispy curl of her bright orange hair and said, "I think we've got another box to do." The Diamondbacks fan didn't look Marissa in the eye, nor did Sheila.

Marissa sat down. You put three inserts into each envelope: the local candidate on top, then the presidential one, with the half-slip voter's guide used as a holder.

"So," Marissa said, having put together her third packet, "it's a pretty exciting time. I can feel it in the air."

The man in the Diamondbacks cap looked at her from over the gold rim of his glasses. He gave her what seemed to be a profoundly sad smile. "Can you? Yeah."

Sheila was watching C-SPAN through the cutout in the wall.

"Do you think we're going to win?"

"Anything's possible."

"Well, that's what we're here for, isn't it?" Marissa pursued. "It's time for a change."

"Charlie here's been looking for a change for thirty-two years," Sheila said, pursing her pinked-out lips. She was collating the packets without looking down, yet somehow they were in perfect order.

"Wow, thirty-two years?"

"Yuppers."

"That's cool."

"Hey, Sheila, any more guides over there? We're plum out," Charlie said, patting the table, looking at the wall above Marissa's head.

Sheila riffled around the box at her feet, then handed him a few more.

It turned out Marissa could leave before the end of the seven-to-ten shift, because they finally did run out of voter's guides. She looked around the room for that one woman a final time, but didn't see her.

"So, do I just go?" she asked Charlie. "Is there anything more I can do?"

He was winding his watch. "Take it as manna from heaven. No more work to do, time to go home," he said, not smiling, per se, but giving her a look that she could tell was meant to be kind.

Today must have been someone's birthday. A half-eaten sheet cake was out by the pamphlets on the front table, a sweet, soft skeleton key to an invisible door.

The bar was pleasing, comforting as a fireplace in a cabin in the woods in the winter. This was a nice antidote to the darkness at the edge of the city, or the darkness of Marissa's own room, which loomed in her consciousness like the thought balloon of someone with nothing to say.

Two brothers from Alpha Beta Psi—Matt and Joey—sat at the booth with her, plus Katy from Chi Chi Delta, who lived across the hall from Marissa and had hooked up with Joey during pledge week. The Katy-and-Joey creation myth included the frat's rooftop and a high-end bottle of cherry vodka.

Matt was cute, a junior, except he *always* thought about football. As Marissa talked about how the fall election was going to be a game changer, he held his draft steady, as if in defense against planetary tremors. His eyes were also still, and reflected in their darkness and stillness was a mini high-res image, teensy-weensy fellows hustling across his corneas, throwing dust motes. They hustled in one direction, and then back again.

Eventually Matt lifted his beer and took a long, slow drink. He put the forty-eight-ounce mug down and said, "That's cool, I guess. But is it even true you can count political volunteering toward your pledge? I don't think so."

The Chi Chis and the "Strongmen" from Alpha Beta Psi were working together on a car wash/taco stand fund-raiser a week from Friday, the last of many gigs they'd paired up on this year. Hanging out with these guys was inevitable—and fun. The fact remained that forming friendships was a tenet and goal of Greek life, in addition to helping build community and doing right by those less fortunate than oneself.

Marissa was an optimist. She'd always been thus, even as a small child, when "optimist" was an extra-credit vocabulary word and her parents chuckled about her getting points for knowing it, really knowing it, inside herself. It was probably optimism that led her to this current presidential candidate—she actually kind of had a crush on him. It was probably optimism that had led her to the sorority and helped convince her as she read the Chi Chi Delta mission statement.

She *did*, very much, like to belong, but who didn't? And she'd already gotten a lot out of being a sister. She'd made friends quickly—more than she'd made her whole freshman year. At this point she could, if she chose to, drink tea and make conversation with any number of other girls in their very own, pretty cool living room. She was going to lots of parties and doing good works. You could say she was part of something bigger. (This went on, too, past graduation, said the housemother. A Chi Chi had a lifetime network, a guaranteed community.) And it's not like she *wasn't* herself when she was in the group—in the pack of girls parading down Cherry in matching minidresses and high heels and straightened hair.

"Sure you can. Right, Katy?"

"Right what?"

Katy had one hand on Joey, under the table, and the other hand on her pink phone. Though she was wearing a velour pantsuit much like Marissa's, she'd dressed it up with diamond bar earrings and a matching necklace: three thin columns, a disassembled delta.

"Volunteering for Obama counts for the house, right? I volunteered for almost three hours tonight."

"Oh," said Katy. She scrunched her eyebrows. "I don't know. Is it cool?" she finally said, answering the question with a question.

"I don't know. I mean it doesn't *totally* matter. I'm glad I did it no matter what."

"It's so fucked up," Matt said, firmly of an opinion now. "You can't do that, Marissa."

"Yes, she can," said Joey, the wiry, ringleader type. "James did. He was like, going door to door, being the kind of pain in the ass that comes naturally to him. Because of James, the lunatic Dems will probably get elected and do their best to plow this country under again."

"I love James," said Katy, knocking into Joey's shoulder with her own.

"Here we go," said Joey. "Waiter, get me a Sex on the Beach. Three Sex on the Beaches. Shit, now!"

"Sex on the Beach?" said Matt. "Jack and Coke, dude. What are you, a douche-bag?"

"Like I care where someone volunteers—hello! Long as it doesn't mess with the part*ay*." Joey raised his glass, and both Katy and Marissa clinked.

Matt was getting more and more disturbed, though. Football aside, he'd begun to take special interest in Marissa these past days, or maybe two weeks. "Isn't it kind of—nerdy, or useless? I mean, like, politics? What the fuck? That's as bad as . . . I don't know."

"We take our community efforts seriously over at Chi, you know that," said Katy. "We care."

"Yeah, we care," said Marissa.

"I care," said Joey, looking at Katy in a meaningful manner.

Matt was dumbfounded. He checked his phone and went back to watching the television mounted over the bar, nestled above a row of specialty vodkas and taps for two faux microbrews, as well as Bud Light and plain Budweiser. Eventually Marissa's eyes drifted over in that direction, in part because Matt was staring, and also because she really could use, if not a Sex on the Beach or a Jack and Coke, another beer.

Caught at an angle, the candidate's headquarters filled the screen, the building where she'd been earlier that night. A woman in a pink trench coat was standing before the entrance, about where Marissa had parked. Behind her was a web of yellow tape, and splashing over her were emergency lights, *wheeeeeerrr wheeeeeerrr wheeeeeerrr*. The headline read: *Deadly Explosion Local Dem Hdqtrs*. A second headline read: *One Dead in Downtown Blast. Action Team Update Breaking Story*.

"Oh my God."

"What's up?" said Katy.

"See that? What is that?"

Katy stretched to see the screen. She looked back at Marissa. "What?"

"Something happened. Here—let me out."

Matt slid out of the booth and stood, all the while continuing a conversation with Joey about the Raiders' draft prospects.

When Marissa returned, she just stood there for a minute, like a server waiting for their order. "Oh my God," she said again.

"What happened?" said Katy.

"There was an explosion. Someone was killed. Where I was, an hour ago."

"Jesus," said Joey. "That's fucked up."

"You could have been killed. That would have messed up everything," said Matt.

"Marissa!" pleaded Katy, as if Marissa could make it all right, turn back time and make this unpleasantness disappear.

Marissa wanted to say, "What is the world coming to?" but that would have been too much like her mother, or maybe her grandmother. She felt her palms tingling, as if she were growing metallic hairs. The worst was real, the threat of violence widespread. "They don't know if it was a bomb, or what. It could have been. It could have been a political act."

Katy turned to Joey now, giving him the same imploring look she'd given Marissa.

He took the cue. "Come back, Rissa, come finish your beer."

"Come on, babe," Matt said, patting the bench next to him.

Marissa reluctantly sat down again. Matt put his arm around her, and over the next half hour, he consoled her with the thought that it might have been an accident, or if it hadn't been, then it was some sorry-ass lone bomber, not any kind of conspiracy, not any larger plot of significance. Marissa could not stop thinking about who might have been killed. The pink-clad newscaster had said the identity of the person was being kept private until family was notified. Was it the lady with the braid, who had said *wunderbar* and was angular and stern and had almost completely disregarded her? Was it the young revolutionary—or so she had come to think of the tall guy with his phone, the quiet, committed type? Or the ponytail girl, maybe his girlfriend? Or the comical old woman—in her denim and smeared makeup? Was it the sad Diamondbacks fan, with the white mustache and the reserved smile? Who had been a volunteer forever—his name was Charlie—a volunteer for thirty-two years?

"It's unfair," she said.

"You're dealing with a shock, Marissa," Katy said, more confident now in her consolation. "Of course it feels unfair."

"Fortify the perimeters of the castle. What say you, Matt?" Joey said in a pirate accent. "The natives are prowling—they're getting a hold of the explosives now."

"They're genuinely fucking around with the excellence of our afternoon," Matt said, rising to the occasion.

"Or evening," said Joey, shrugging.

"Or evening," Matt conceded.

Her companions wanted to go to a party back at the frat, but Marissa said she didn't know what she wanted to do. They were standing outside the bar on University, the street a festive outreach of campus life, so brightly lit you couldn't see any stars at all.

The news said someone had called in and taken responsibility for the explosion, but that claim was still unverified.

She felt numb overall, aware of two competing sensations. One was hinged on the idea that this catastrophe, this possibly malignant action, was like a *Cops* episode, no big deal *really*, more like an adventure—the times of our lives, what's in the news, et cetera. But there was also this other sensation, an unscripted, ransacking, glass-shard feeling.

As the four discussed who would go with whom and would Marissa come or not, a group of theater types appeared, having run over from the other side of the street. Traveling minstrels, they seemed to consider themselves: a man wearing a green velvet hat with three curved horns, black tights, and purple One Stars; another man with dreadlocks, much hardware around his ears and nose, his skin the color of a blue raspberry

ICEE; a woman in a shredded wedding gown holding a parasol, her face painted like a skeleton; a second woman, who at first Marissa thought was a child she was so small, wearing a green and purple striped tunic and a hippie skirt. She was holding a scepter with a pig's face on top.

"If only she had somebody there to shoot her every minute of her life," shrieked the man with the blue face, twisting his body and yowling right at Marissa and her three friends. "Every day, every minute of her life."

"Things would have been *sooooooo* good," said the tiny striped woman, jumping toward and then away from Marissa.

"Everything would have been just fine!" said the bride.

"They would have been *divine*," screamed the blue man.

The thespian quartet ran on to harass the next group of normals on the sidewalk.

Marissa stood frozen in Tucson's balmy night.

"People like that shouldn't even be *allowed*," Katy said.

"People?" scoffed Matt, watching them disappear into the crowd. "Let's get out of here. High and dry of all this douche-baggery. C'mon."

"I don't think I'm going to go," Marissa said. "I'm just going to call it a night."

"Baby, you need company after your close call . . . with death!" said Katy, eyes wide. Then, more confidentially, "Besides, I can't handle these two alone."

It wasn't completely clear how serious she was, but Marissa was sensitive to the idea of solidarity, companionship. And so she went to the party at what they termed the "frat castle." The stench of beer was a kind of modern-day potpourri, getting the mood right. Though it didn't feel so modern after all—it felt almost medieval in the darkened room, the thumping bass zapping over to a narcotic whine zapping over to a duet. Corners alive with dark forms. It seemed quite clear to Marissa that she wasn't at all drunk enough, and that it was really all right for her to feel her individual sorrows, here among all the others who didn't seem to have any sorrows at all.

But the others *did* have sorrows, didn't they? Didn't everyone?

Matt lumbered over, and she accepted a beer from him. He was wearing the same polo shirt as all the other men in the room. They enlisted into this conscription, a little like the sorority sisters in their cocktail dresses or their velour. But there could be variety in polo shirts; everyone had his own color. Matt's was maroon.

"I like this song," she said.

"Rocks," Matt said, his head bobbing in time-honored fashion. Joey and Katy were nowhere to be seen.

Marissa's gaze fell upon another Chi Chi across the room. She was petite, like the girl in the thespian horror show, attired in a soft pink sweater and a black cami with glittering studs around the neckline. Her straight, preternaturally thin legs wobbled this then that way, as if she were on a boat—though all the while she remained rooted in place, black velvet flats steady. Two young men were fucking with her, Marissa could tell from here, even if she couldn't hear what they said.

"Hey," she said to Matt.

"Hey what, pretty girl?"

She didn't know what she was going to say, but then her mouth was moving, deliberately forming words. "My dad always said that the two-party system is what makes this country work. The two parties—they disagree, and because of that, each is made stronger."

"What the fuck are you talking about?" He looked down at her. Even the football players had gone into stasis.

"I'm just saying."

"You're a strange chick, you know that?"

Matt patted her butt then and said something else, but she couldn't hear what it was. In any case, they dropped the subject.

A lot of time elapsed, and at some point she and Katy talked about death—how freaking *weird* it was—and at another point, Matt captured her by the back of her velour pants and led her into the bathroom and they fucked around for a little while, although they didn't get too far. The touching was odd—like using a hand towel or a worry stone—so somehow that didn't even really seem to count as a sexual act. The actual towel rack jutted into Marissa's back as Matt tried to find his way, a hopeless truffle hunter, into the small section of exposed Marissa, between her pulled-down panties and the bottom of her shirt.

She decided not to wait for Katy to go home.

The retail stores were closed by this time, past midnight, though a couple of restaurants were open, and people still walked in twos and threes down the sidewalk. At Urban Outfitters, festoons of silver garland fell upon the shoulders of mannequins, their perky breasts nippleless, "perky" being the word her English professor had used last semester to describe Marissa's own boobs. God! That was the epitome of awful—although she knew, or she'd hoped, he didn't mean anything by it. Still, that was one of those isolated moments when it was Marissa and Marissa alone trying to figure out what to do next. As it turned out, the professor just kept talking, and she was left with a smirk or a grimace, that was all, and then her smile fell like a paper umbrella in the rain, like the worst cake ever baked by a drunken housewife.

Sex was part of the equation, obviously. Sex was part of the equation at Chi Chi Delta and Alpha Beta Psi. Sex was exceptionally isolating, and yet even so, here it was, kind of a club. In high school, she'd slept with two guys—one in her junior year, one in her senior year. She'd stayed with Jesse and then Rick for months, and she was still friends with Rick. She'd doubled that number now . . . tripled it, actually. In almost two years of college, she'd learned and tried to unlearn four fellows.

Marissa wondered where the theater people had gone. Did they live in some velvet/sequin squalor, did they do drugs (as her parents would no doubt imagine)? In Katy and Matt and Joey's world, they almost didn't exist at all—nor did the activist types downtown, nor the whole Activist Room, nor Saturday's rally either. *Chimera*, the English professor might have said, before ogling her perky self. No one at the party had even known about the explosion, and so it was Marissa who had brought them the news. She'd looked into their eyes and held her beer carefully out to one side and told them that she'd almost *died*. That someone *did* die. It could have been Charlie, or Sheila.

Walking along the illuminated avenue, Marissa leaned into a small wind. A gray feeling filled her ears, the aftershock of music at the frat castle. She felt cold between her legs, as if she'd just taken off a scarf or bandage. She hoped she'd never see Matt again. She thought this quickly, furiously, and just as quickly, she stopped thinking it. A pragmatist as well as an optimist, she realized she certainly *would* see him again, if not before, then at the taco sale/car wash next weekend. She still didn't know if her volunteer work at the Democratic headquarters would count toward her monthly tally, but now she really didn't care. Anyway, it didn't look like she'd be going back there—wherever the new headquarters would be, some temporary location. Moderate Republican or not, her father would have a conniption fit if she went back now.

Marissa walked all the way down University to Park, then right on Cherry to Sorority Row. She'd been walking quickly, wanting to get there, but after she'd gone up the path and the two steps to Chi Chi Delta, she stopped close to the door, weaving like the black-slippered girl at the frat. She didn't want to go in. She didn't want to go into the living room where there might be someone waiting, wanting to talk. She didn't want to wake up tomorrow and go with Sara and Aubrey to pick up the T-shirts at the garment-manufacturing place, and she didn't want to network, or party, or do good works, or be a sister. She didn't want to talk about death, or see any overblown expressions of concern and amazement at her close call. She didn't want to talk to any frat boys at any frat parties, ever again. Because there were other boys out there—Rick wasn't a frat boy, for instance. It was true! You didn't have to be a frat boy. You didn't have to be a sorority sister. You could sleep outside, far from Sorority Row, you could sleep in some squalid black place—where the theater people slept, what they called home—or you could sleep in South Tucson where she'd almost gotten lost earlier. You could sleep out on a bench, all by yourself, and look up at the night, and watch the stars.

At the Spa

Alyssa experiences pleasure. The unknown girl is nudging all around the periphery of her body, the girl's fist a little thump against the bamboo blanket in which Alyssa is entombed. The girl moves down Alyssa's arm, hip, leg, and feet (giving them more of a jiggle than a nudge), then back up the other leg, the other arm, landing at Alyssa's head—the center of most problems.

And yet with the extremely sad and majestic Celtic-inspired music being piped in, the consciousness of one hour still to go, and the lingering scent of lavender and ylang-ylang in the air, the troubles that usually afflict Alyssa do not stay in her head for long. The troubling thought enters, but instead of capturing her, it drifts back out again. Only to be followed by another. Still they come gently, these shades of troubles. They don't have their regular vigor, their fight instinct.

It's not exactly trouble, but one of the reoccurring thought patterns Alyssa is cycling through is a set of speculations about the girl herself, the aesthetician. Whose hands *are* these? This soft thumping.

Alyssa is not "to the manner born," and this is the third spa treatment she's ever had—the other two were stringer activities at weddings, the expensive fun of being a bridesmaid, which she has been, often. Alyssa works forty or fifty hours a week. She does not own her car. She rents an apartment. Her parents are still working, both of them: her father as a commercial/residential contractor and her mother as the manager of a small corporate cleaning company. Alyssa doesn't receive financial support from them (well, she's twenty-seven—why should she?), and she doesn't have any pots of money lying around, spoils from obscure connections or lucky investments. Although now, for two years actually, Alyssa has been making what she'd consider, or what she'd *once* have considered, a good paycheck, working as executive assistant to the director of Communications at Raytheon. At first she got a bit of a breathless feeling, looking at the figure in the "gross pay" box. Now, either the cost of everything is going up, or Alyssa has taken on more expenses, or her debts are coming due. It doesn't seem quite as much as before.

Still the heft of the check is an affirmation of rightness, of what she's chosen to do, of where she's gotten so far. She amounts to something, literally. She *almost* amounts to something.

And Alyssa's good at what she does. She takes pride in her work. Neither peacenik nor warmonger, she understands that countries need defense, and defense requires weaponry. Someone has to make the weapons, and the better the weapons, the better, period. For everyone, for the country. Certainly at Raytheon there is an overall ethos of pride, even honor, though most days, most weeks even, she doesn't talk weapons with anyone (she talks press releases, and even if the press release is about a weapons system, this feels far removed from the tactile implications of steel, depleted uranium, C-4)—or not often, anyway. There was that eager, fairly handsome dude from Engineering. He had a thrilled look when he cornered her in the kitchen, giving her a penny-for-your-thoughts, unasked-for disquisition on the AIM-9X, which they were in the process of updating. Quite a thrilled look. The thrill in his blue eyes, as he gazed above her head and over to the supply cabinet. The way his muscles twitched slowly and with some kind of methodical pulsing action under his crisp white shirt.

Zero hadn't mentioned weapons to her. Not the first time, nor since. Zero was simultaneously above weapons and so infused with weapons, so very much *of the weapon*, there was very little reason for him to talk about them at all.

The girl's hands insist, release. FedEx never found the report for Dallas even though she had the tracking number—why, and what could Alyssa have done about it? Had she miswritten the address? Her brother and his wife and the Fourth of July, still not resolved and so very reminiscent of everything that had come before, everything they'd done and how much of a hash their relationship apparently was. Her knee, the necessity for a second opinion. The issue with the bill from the dermatologist. The fact that she is sleeping with another woman's husband, and that this other woman, embarrassingly, is suffering from breast cancer.

Nothing lodges, nothing stays, Alyssa is a way station. She lets herself think again—if you can *let* yourself think—about the woman whose hands are under her neck and shoulders, rubbing in a professional yet intimate way, now under her shoulder blade, the *nudge nudge nudge* a set of firm commas—that's how she'd have to describe it—rubbing her underside, the dark below, the weight of Alyssa's own body creating the pressure.

The girl could be her slave. The girl could be her lover. Alyssa could be a queen, and girls like this could do her bidding, could attend to her, whenever she wanted. She could be a very, very wealthy wife, recipient of facials and massages every Friday afternoon, a much-needed relief from the tensions of the week, the tensions of being alive, the tensions of any life but her life in particular.

But the girl is just an aesthetician with her own life to lead, her own paycheck to work for. It's wrong to indulge in slave fantasies, Alyssa thinks, slammed back to this reality, as the girl whips up a batch of clay for the mask, the whisking sound almost like her mother's whisking of batter at home, or something equally mundane. The facial/minimassage is probably half over. Alyssa won't be coming back to the Chartreuse Retreat & Spa right away, though she can't *completely* rule out another indulgence such as this in her future, thanks to Zero. So nice of him to present her with the gift certificate—he's always so nice to her. He felt bad that he'd been distracted, he knew he'd been out of it lately, not really there—and so in a sense, this slave girl's hands are an extension of his hands, those latter hands being dry, cupped, hard, and yet capable, too, in their own way.

She could like a girl such as this one, with hands that are soft but also firm. There's something about women, the softness being part of it, and the capacity for kinship, for really *knowing* one another. But Alyssa has to admit she likes the cleanness of this transaction—she's getting what she paid for (or Zero paid for), and she has no emotional entanglement with this girl at all.

Later, in the Tranquility Room, where the ladies in their white robes recline between services, drinking cucumber water, Alyssa closes her eyes, *Vogue* still clasped in her hands, open to an ad for a pelt. She is thinking about something the yoga teacher said, yoga being one of the classes offered during one's Day of Beauty. "A little discomfort is fine, we can expect discomfort at the place of transformation, and this is our goal today, to let ourselves go to that place. But don't let it get to the point of *insistent* pain. We stop before insistent pain," the lithe instructor murmured, walking (toe first, like an Indian princess) between the student practitioners, just then buckled over and halfway splayed.

Where is the line between discomfort and pain? This is something Alyssa wondered at the time, her right leg extended behind her as far as it could go, arms raised to the sun, back arched, and the smile on her face ("A smile releases endorphins all on its own, you know") a bit grimace-y overall. There was a certain amount of discomfort in her relationship with Zero. Because she had been brought up to be honest. (Isn't everyone *brought up* to be honest? Surely half the world's parents aren't encouraging subterfuge.) Or let's say a kind of honesty felt essential to Alyssa's well-being, her sense of self. It was truly lovely, riveting, fucking exciting, when he said what he said at the team-building seminar, and it has been lovely ever since, the half-dozen dinners, a few tumbles back at her house, twice at La Paloma. She remembers when he told her of his wife's illness. The tiramisu had just arrived, and they both had a gleaming fork at the ready, and the server had bowed and shuffled backward and then turned into a puff of smoke. "The truth is Hanna has been dealing with health issues lately, Alyssa. She has breast cancer. She's getting treatment now, but it's been hard for her, for us both, of course." He kept his eyes on her while he spoke—not exactly looking *into* her eyes, but at her right earring, or so it seemed. His voice was vulnerable—yes, that is the word she used to describe it to herself. He was being honest with her.

When she stroked his cock later that night, her delicate hand reaching over the oxblood console between the front seats of his car, over the stretch of pale, soft leather and across his casual, albeit pressed, khakis, reaching into the nook of his Brooks Brothers (or so she imagined—she hadn't looked at the label!) boxers, the eroticism of the moment was tempered by curiosity about the wife and her condition, and when the wife might have last touched this same penis, and when the wife and Zero might have last eaten tiramisu, and if the radiation was affecting her appetite at this point, and if she'd lost her hair.

But the truth is, by and large, Alyssa has been able to put the wife into perspective. Does her dalliance with Zero—for she isn't in love, nor is he, she doesn't think he is, not exactly—constitute anything, *any* kind of action upon Hanna at all? In some ways, not. She's not real to Hanna, and so it's as if she has carte blanche, an independent life. If Hanna doesn't know about Alyssa and what she's doing with Zero, then all that is happening between them is happening in an alternate universe. It's a non-reality.

Just as Hanna is a non-reality for her.

But then out of the gentle eucalyptus bloom of the slightly misted air, from the last chaise lounge in the row of four on this side of the Tranquility Room, comes a voice that feels rather painstakingly *like* reality, a harsh reality that should not be allowed in, should not be allowed even *near*, the Tranquility Room. To hear this particular voice impedes upon the fulfillment of tranquility and beauty, severely, for Alyssa.

First the door opened, and there was a shuffle and the murmur of another aesthetician or masseuse, someone droning on about the comfort of the blankets, how they're made of bamboo and how cozy they are, and then this inconsequential someone used the words, "Mrs. Daitch," and there was a puffing of pillows and that was when the second woman said, "Thank you, that's fine, honey." And now the voice remains, an object in Alyssa's ear.

She remains motionless, eyes closed, but something is occurring under her plush and theoretically sustainable robe, which is that she is becoming a cold, drafty, metallic board. If she keeps her eyes shut, can she become invisible? Can she exist fully in a world of darkness, can she actually be *in the dark*? Quite horribly, with an intensity matching that which she experienced under the aesthetician's tender hands, she is experiencing Mrs. Daitch now, as she continues her conversation with the drone, an inquiry about magazines and then cucumber water. When Mrs. Zero Daitch says she prefers home magazines, it's clear she has turned her head toward Alyssa, because the deep, slightly tragic notes pound at Alyssa like pelted snowballs. I'm not myself, Alyssa thinks. In this white robe with my hair swirled up and hidden into the recesses of this towel, and in this unlikely environment—not an office party, not a hotel room—the true self of me is gone, unrecognizable.

You could even say that her face is a mask—perhaps everyone's is. And underneath this face, or mask, Alyssa begins to experience a new sense of the world, a cup-half-empty-at-very-best reality, completely at odds with the Chartreuse Retreat & Spa. Although her skin has been recently slathered with a ylang-ylang concoction by the soft white hands of an underpaid female with a murmuring voice, a slave girl, her skin feels not supple but oily, as if it has been dipped in gasoline. Behind shut eyelids, in the self of herself, Alyssa knows that Mrs. Zero Daitch is looking at her. She is looking through Alyssa's skin and into the butcher's sink of her innards, sloshing dark purple gourds and tubers. The acupressure performed by the talcum-powdered beauty has been rendered null and void. There is no alignment within. It is all black laundry now, juices disgorged, a smell you wouldn't even believe. Her skeleton is brittle, no longer a kind architecture, the armature of survival, but a sad puppet's wooden holder, a thing, a broomstick holding her stiff there on the chaise in the Tranquility Room, jamming her chin and forcing a grinding action at the base of her neck, as if it will grind itself up, and then pop, and there will roll her head, with all its ill will and worries, its sense of order and hunger for pleasure. No such desire now—because even desire begins in the imagination, and with Mrs. Daitch's slow breathing two chaises over, her swift flip of the décor magazine's pages, her boring eyes, imagination has been exiled.

Alyssa would near trade anything to be ejected now, to be gone, out, no Alyssa. Consciousness—maybe life—isn't a joke, but it *is* a trick, mean and thin as a shadow, and there is no glamour in it, no *you can't be too rich or too thin*, no treats or prizes or presents to come. The past is a damp half-used matchbook, and the future is a puff of nothing, a false promise. All the bright stars and all the soft pillows are lost to her—but even the loss is not fully felt, because to feel loss is to cherish, to feel loss is to believe that you might have been or could be again a vessel of love and life, that you hadn't actually been complicit in relegating and cheapening and ob-scuring and overlooking—before it was too late, before the end. Because now *is* too late. The too-lateness is here. The too-lateness is in the oil slick of ylang-ylang, the cucumber in the cucumber water gone foul, the world music—Mrs. Daitch's favorite kind, Zero had once told her—soured, like an old LP playing too slow, whining. Even Mrs. Daitch is nothing; even she is not a Florence Nightingale figure or a heroine. Mrs. Zero Daitch who sees Alyssa, who sees and smells and hates her, even Mrs. Daitch is but a specter and a nothing. It, everything, the demonstration of love, is gone. Alyssa's eyes open.

STORY

Rock

The storm had just begun when Tom entered the church. From the second pew, he could hear rain on the roof, tapping fingers, and then finally more like some drenching drumbeat from *King Kong*. The spattering on the windows was sporadic and high-pitched, on a different aural plane than the roof rain and the distant but intense sound of unfettered water falling, as if from a bucket, over the front eaves and down upon the slate slab at the entrance of the building. He himself had entered without asking. He entered with hope that he could find help here, though he wasn't entirely sure it was all right to just come in like this, despite his job, but then again he figured it probably was. Outside the wide-open doors, the stormy world shone a vivid gray and green, stinging with the smell of mesquite.

The top of the pew pressed into his spine, and his heavy black shoes were jammed against the upturned kneeler. As a boy, Tom felt claustrophobic in cars—he was always too big for small or even medium-sized spaces. His body simply panicked, tightness overtaking his ankles and knees, a sense of collision, of terrible, doomed consequence. Now the feeling swept through him like a black bird. Mostly he'd come to experience this anxiety as a minor inconvenience, just one of many, or to put it another way, he had bigger fish to fry.

God is all.

You had to admit the words had a nice ring to them. He ought to write the phrase in the desert sand. He could piece together a large version with palm fronds, then swing his arms and jump—a passing airplane could save him. But no. No grand gestures for Tom, just the squeezing of himself into this pew, just a matter of getting out of the rain (or off the grid) for a few minutes after last bell, after even the intramural and after-care kids had gone home. And on this Friday in early April, though he'd taught at St. Bart's for eight months, he still wasn't completely sure of the protocol here, the relationships between school, parish, and parents (and children, naturally, at the center of everything), though he *could* tell you that some of the women, these mothers, frightened him more than anything had since—since Halloween 1982. Plain and utterly frightening, and if his own mother were well, he would have told her about them, and she would have said something sarcastic and satisfying. Or he'd be telling Carrie, if she were talking to him.

In the end, Tom realized the headmaster was like anyone else, just trying to get along. He wore the requisite goofy ties of all K–8 administrators. He stood with his hands on his hips and surveyed the scene every weekday morning, his gaze just inches above the cars of the wealthy few tooling around the circular driveway to let off their loads: little boys and girls in burgundy shirts and tan pants, shorts, or skirts. At the fall festival, he'd dressed like the wizard Dumbledore, pretending to light candles with his breath, to have the capacity to turn back time.

This church was made for little people. Midgets. Tom sat as still as he possibly could. He had nowhere to put his hands.

"The point is I don't think I'm getting through to her. I mean, I've tried. I certainly *have* tried. And she's not a dimwit, I know that, I know she understands. The fact of the matter is, I think she's purposely—Bye, sweetheart, bye, bye—"

At 7:47 that morning, Laurabell Daitch retrieved her belongings from the backseat of the car as her mother continued a conversation on her cell phone. "I know, I know, she is *purposely* ignoring my needs here—" She heaved the pack up on one shoulder and, with the hand not holding her lunch bag, swooshed shut the door to the powder blue Lexus, twin to her father's oxblood model, sealing her mother in the perfect symmetry of her own chatter. Eight-year-old Laurabell was set loose upon the world.

She humped toward the fourth-grade courtyard, passing a few middle schoolers standing around the door to the music room. They were tall and well put-together. The girls' hair was brushed within an inch of its life, and the boys had wide shoulders and sleepy mouths. Laurabell shifted her gaze so they wouldn't see that she was looking, or had looked away either. She passed a classmate and the classmate's mother having a tête-à-tête near 4B's front door. This particular mother was wearing medical scrubs, platform shoes, and makeup. Her own mother also took pains with how she looked, but she didn't work at an office or hospital or anything like that. She was a design consultant: clothes, houses, yards. And she had her volunteer work with that special doctor and also with a foundation—something for women, Laurabell thought. *Yeah, I'm going to a committee meeting for the fucking Foundation—and what part of that isn't important? Doesn't anything compute outside of Raytheon? Is Raytheon the whole fucking world?*

It was not pleasant when her mother swore, but she and her father had a pact that each time it happened, he'd give Laurabell a dollar. So, for instance, the fight about her mother's Thursday meeting yielded two dollars, and two dollars, Laurabell thought dully, got her that much closer to the Webkins yellow duck she currently favored.

Tom Williams, Mr. Williams to her, was standing by the SMART Board with his hands clasped behind his back, looking down at one of her classmates. Jason Gant was getting another talking to. Laurabell dropped her lunch bag into the tub by the front door and then walked to her desk and proceeded to take things out of her backpack. You unpacked the notebooks and the textbooks and the homework folder and put them either under your chair or in your desk, and then you put your backpack in your cubby and went back to your desk to finish up any homework or do whatever small thing like that you could until first bell, unless it had already rung, which was the case as often as not, since they were often running late.

Laurabell put her backpack in the cubby and went back to her seat. When she was taking out her spelling exercise book from the shelf under her desk, a note fell out. *You cant come to my birthday party because your mom is a hore!*

Finally, there is forgiveness, thought Tom. It would come, like a terrifying roar. And yet sometimes forgiveness abandoned you, abandoned everyone, and the stale smell of last week's frankincense and myrrh was all that remained, the extinguished candles and the echo of the organ from Sunday's High Mass in a church empty except for the sound of the rain coming from all angles, from everywhere.

The job had seemed so good, back at his interview with the headmaster—who was filled with grand and egalitarian ideas and asked Tom important questions, as he told Carrie later—and in his first conversations with the other teachers, a collection of exceptionally talented, if also weary, individuals. He'd never worked at a private school before. My God, eighteen kids in a class? He could actually *teach* here, rather than the constant struggle that had become public education back home (before the layoffs, that is, his included). The pay differential didn't seem too bad once you factored in Tucson's cost of living, and at first he and Carrie were both prepared to move—excited about moving—halfway across the country, away from friends, family, all they'd known. He'd finally be able to make his astronomy club a reality, too—a dream since he himself was in school. Eight-year-olds! How incredible they all were, teetering on the far side of childhood, those precious days and weeks before they realized what a shit-ass world we live in. No, that's not what he meant. No, life was amazing. And teaching was like waiting tables at the busiest restaurant in town; it was almost like being a priest yourself. You were offering a sense of the world as a place a kid could have faith in—a place where she could fit in, play a role. Not a role as a victim, as a *hore*.

His first day at St. Bart's, he and Carrie had fought in the morning—morning arguments being perhaps the most awful of the subspecies *argumenta*. She said she doubted he even *wanted* children. What? You can know something intellectually, and it never matters. By then she'd already told him she absolutely fucking loathed the desert, and it didn't matter that he'd promised they would spend summers with her family in Wisconsin and that he'd take over cooking every other night and do the laundry, too. And it certainly didn't help, in this liking the desert business, that she'd had her second miscarriage literally *on the way into town*. She was sitting in the passenger seat of the U-Haul, Rihanna on the radio, and she felt something, apparently, because the next minute she was putting her hand down her pants, and then she was staring at him, holding her hand up like a stop sign, five fingers splayed, blood on two of them.

Their condo was cute, in a southwestern kind of way. Neither of them much liked the austere tile floor. Their voices echoed when they were unpacking (or he was unpacking, and she was crying, sometimes in the bathroom, sometimes in a chair). He didn't even mention what had to have been a roadrunner pecking around on their patio—this big, bitchy-looking bird with a fanned-out tail. It would have been stupid—irrelevant. Their bad luck had followed them twelve hundred miles. What good was a bird to her now?

But she still had the anthropology program, with the track in archaeology. It wasn't like anthropology had been her passion for a *long* time, but it did fall into the realm of something to do. She needed something to do. According to the website, the goal of the program was "to find real answers about what it means to be human, where we come from, and where we'll be in the future." Which was good. A little science-fiction-y, a little kitsch. But all in all, something they could use.

That was eight months ago, before the notion of infidelity started cracking their marriage like ice or an egg or the desert floor. It wasn't infidelity itself—or it was, for all he knew—but the sense that what had been magnificent was presently flawed, could be broken down into composite parts, useless in themselves.

The mothers stand outside the door. And some of the mothers were perfectly nice, could even be friends, he supposed, if he and Carrie were gathering friends, were in harvest mode. And all the mothers were unique, no doubt, God's creations, yet when they stand outside the door, they become a unit that Tom finds, at least, formidable. Two weeks ago, one of them stepped forward from the clutch and pulled him aside. She smiled broadly, holding his arm. He did not care for this (remember the claustrophobia), but he did his best not to freak out while she told him of the "big doings" and "series of betrayals" occurring "as we speak." Of course, she knew he had to keep his mind on the most important things, the things that really matter, that are at the center of it all—the children, of course. But if he could also just *think* about the problem, and *consider*, you know, the implications, and what should be done next. They didn't want to overreact, but they now felt compelled. It was time to go to the school board. Vote of no confidence, maybe. Call in an accountant, a new development officer, the accreditation people? Tom listened, his shoes sinking into the paving stones before his classroom as if into slow mud. This mother's son was a mop-headed fellow, brilliant blond hair, who just the day before had been surprised to learn that bats were not birds but mammals, and it had made Tom smile to see the boy's eyes widen in amazement at this fact. The mother now whispered, even more sinisterly and conspiratorially, "One of the meanest of the bunch has a daughter in your class. It's a tragedy, I tell you. It has got to be stopped."

Dutifully—naively?—he reported the conversation to the headmaster. The headmaster had his hands clasped before him on the desk. He shook his head when Tom wondered aloud if they should do something about it, if perhaps the mothers were, in a way, running the place—like inmates running the asylum, Tom joked, only not so much the actual *inmates*, who were fairly cute, but a relentless gang of underemployed,

Botoxed warriors. At this, the headmaster blanched. "We're not going there," he said, touching his funny tie. He offered no coherent analysis of the highly involved parents and their feuds, *Lord of the Flies* meets *Mommie Dearest*. Not that Tom felt he needed *much*, he just wanted a smoothly running classroom, and he wanted the band of mothers to get away from his door.

Now Laurabell. "What does this mean?" she'd asked that morning, handing him the note. She was a tired-looking redhead, and she did her own hair. At least he hoped that was the case. Four haphazard pigtails sprung out from her scalp like miniature auburn dusters, or dead robin tail feathers.

The church had a raw beauty—as if faith were etched out of some cave, and all the delineations of civilization were but a series of simple lines separating us from chaos. Not a mission itself, St. Bartholomew's was still reminiscent of San Xavier del Bac, the "White Dove of the Desert" in the Tohono O'odham Nation. (Tom and Carrie had gone there, somberly, a week after they got into town. It was a hundred and eight degrees the day they peeled off I-19 to view this unlikely desert-landed Taj Mahal. Desperate characters were selling fried dough in the parking lot, and the gift shop was closed.) St. Bart's was also whitewashed, built low to the ground, adobe puzzle pieces held in place by thick black posts and rails. Inside it was airy but dark, a stark cruciform design with small square windows and a ceiling made from the spines of saguaros. Barbed wreaths marked the Stations of the Cross, seven on the left wall and seven on the right. It was a little bit of agony, looking at them. A corporeal rendering of Christ hung over the altar. To the right, underneath a sculpture of the Holy Mary (her body emanating gilt leaves, or maybe fire), a half-dozen votives flickered.

Her mother was not a "hore," he'd explained to Laurabell. The note was, as the day's language would have it, inappropriate (rage rising up when he used this word, inappropriate its own fucking self). Did she have any idea who it might have come from? Laurabell shook her head. She seemed to recognize that a mistake had been made, that despite the hype and the promise, the world was going wrong.

Tom called Carrie at lunchtime, but she didn't answer. Even if she had, would he have been able to talk to her, given the circumstances? She was a building with thirty windows, all of them shuttered. And so he had decided not to, or he simply couldn't tolerate the idea of, burdening her, as they say, with his *little problems.* The words for all this came at him in a series of bitterly conceived, never-to-be-spoken snippets of conversation. Point, counterpoint, point again. But life was filled with problems such as this, and what made them small anyway? What was small about Laurabell? If Carrie answered—if he told her—she'd probably dispense with the situation in a hurry. In and out, shutters closed. "I told you the rich were a bunch of assholes," she'd said when he first complained about the scary women by his door, as if the eighteen young faces in his classroom were thus rendered null and void.

It was probably a trick of the light, the gradations of darkness sweeping in and out of the church. He was tempted to light a blue candle before the Virgin Mary, at the feet of the woman burning or radiating with sorrow. Or joy. Did you put a quarter in a box? Was it rude to light two? Might he wish there, or complain, or shout, or howl? Before they left for the science lab, he heard the boy with the blond mop-top talking about his party. The kid looked around to where Laurabell was sharpening her pencil, narrowed his eyes, and then went back to talking to his friends. Laurabell revolved the old-fashioned handle, oblivious. And for a few breathless moments, it was as if Tom didn't even like children anymore. The feeling came and went, but afterward, he felt disgusting and exhausted, as if he'd been poisoned. He pulled the boy aside. "Did you leave a note in Laurabell's desk this morning?" A dull fear crossed the kid's face, but then he went back to cock of the walk mode. "Yeah, so what?"

Tom knew the mother would be in the klatch of mothers at the end of the day, as reliable as gravity itself, or the Pythagorean theorem. She was wearing a flowing tan blouse, made of some latter-day gossamer. She held her arms tightly against her chest as he spoke, her lips rising into an otherworldly smile. He was concerned, he'd said, because of the language used, and because of the fragility and importance of classroom dynamics, and because anonymous notes were always a bad idea. Did she know where this language might have come from? He sought her help in thinking this through. He found himself twisting his pen as he spoke, as her smile widened and froze.

"I told you the bad people were everywhere, didn't I?" she hissed, a purely crazy look in her eyes.

"I'm going to be home a little late tonight," he'd said into his wife's voice mail at the end of the school day. Quitting, of course, would have been silly, an incredible overreaction—and yet as he packed his bag, stuffing in papers, he felt blind to anything else, blind to the concept that he could deal with this one more day. Everything was wrong with this town. Everything. So they should move, get the fuck out of here, go back to Kansas City. She could transfer her credits from the year and finish up the master's there. Or they could move to Albuquerque to be near his mother. He could help his mother. They could stay in his old bedroom and he could read the comic books from the basement and drive her to the hospital for her treatments, and he could make it easier, make it better for her, because of course—he thought, as if someone had kicked him, as if some outside force were actually kicking this Houdini suitcase that was his lot, here between one pew and the next—her tumor was serious, after all. And he was far away.

Or *he* could move there, not *they*.

Tom got up from the pew and walked toward the altar. He stood in the center of the aisle, at the mouth of the Oriental carpet that spread down three steps to the stone floor. He let out a breath, and then he took a breath, and another one.

Troubles follow you everywhere, he told himself, walking away from the altar and back toward the front door. Was this a consolation?

He paused by the font of water, maybe holy, and the table of church-related brochures and flyers. A trip to a dinner theater, a ladies' luncheon, a call for food and clothing. The font was nearly empty, but in the bottom was a small, still pool. He touched it with one fingertip, as a branch might. And then he kept walking. He walked right up to the edge of the world, where the rain was coming down in sheets and planes, and stood in the doorway, blinking at the brightness of the storm.

Forge

The boy has never been friends with a black person before. Of course, he hasn't been friends with nearly *anybody* before; his friends are his parents is all. He is thirteen now, which means he is a teenager. He has said this word to himself in his room at night, whispered it in the dark. It's a terrific word.

His room, which is exactly where he wishes he were right now, is the last one down the hall to the right, after the bathroom. The hall light is never on. When you come from the bathroom or from the kitchen, his room shines like a beacon. It's his favorite place in the world. Even his parents knock on the door before coming in. His room is pretty much off-limits to everyone. His mother said that. She said it when they were eating dinner on the couch as a special occasion one weekend. She'd smiled at him and patted his knee and said, "Your room is your own, Elton. That's your safe place, okay?" He'd ducked his head, tried to get back to watching television.

Still the comment stayed with him, adding to the radiant idea that his room was actually and truly a castle of excellence and strength at the end of the hall. (Purple shag carpeting with black triangles and white moons. Flecks of yellow, like stars. Part of the carpet is smashed and old looking, the part near his bed, and also where the aquarium ruptured and spilled water everywhere, as well as fish. Elton laughed at first when he saw the fish on his carpet, the neon tetras and the fat old rainbow fish and the orange guppies and the thin striped danios. On the top bunk, a big pile of stupid PT equipment and some boxes. A desk and a dresser, and a TV of his own.)

So the reason Elton is not lounging in his room at this particular moment in time, which is seeming like a very very very very very very very long moment indeed, is that his parents *thought it would be smart in the long run, this isn't fun and games, Elton,* to follow the doctor's advice. It is and always has been awful when the doctor says things. Doctor words are too powerful. A doctor just *says* something and—and anything could happen after that. It was a doctor who said he was "plump as a bedbug" when he was a little kid. It was a doctor who took his glasses off and looked at Elton's mother and said, "The time is now," and he was talking about the operation then. It was the new doctor, a lady doctor, who had most recently said that the time *wasn't* now, talking about surgery, that they really did need to use common sense here—and plain, honest-to-goodness, old-fashioned exercise was absolutely, 100% essential. "Beneficial six ways from Sunday. Physical, mental—you name it, Mrs. Larsen. We want to do all we can for the poor kid."

"We" being the doctor's way of siding with his parents. Against him.

"Love is like an oyster, Elton, it's like an oyster, I say. Do you know why it's like an oyster?" asks Jenko, hands on his slim hips.

"No," Elton pants. "Why?"

On the second floor of the athletic club, close to the central stairwell so in full view of everyone, the stationary bike is a torture device upon which Elton sits. Jenko set the height of the seat, the function (hill training—Jesus!), duration, and difficulty (starting last week they made it to 3, and in case anyone wants to know, Elton doesn't think this is cool or fun or worthy of respect—so far he just hates 3). Now he stands next to Elton. Ten minutes on the bike, then weights. Then swimming, then the Jacuzzi, then Jenko drives him home. The car was a requirement for the job, which his parents advertised on Craigslist. Jenko and Elton do this on Saturday morning, as well as on Tuesday and Thursday after school. They've been doing it now for almost a month.

Jenko himself, he runs. Doesn't even know what fat is. He's an athlete through and through—that's why he's here, in America. Because he can run so well, because all kinds of places give him trophies and ribbons, because he might even go to the next Olympics. He told Elton this is his dream. Jenko is five foot nine, short for a runner but still taller than Elton. He probably weighs 140 pounds, whereas Elton weighs 224 (Saturday's weight—the Saturday before was 225). Jenko has only been in this country for four years. He's from Kenya. He went someplace in Illinois first and then got a scholarship to come to the University of Arizona. When he got the scholarship, his whole family flew over from Africa to live here. They didn't even know what a dishwasher was, according to Jenko, which made Elton laugh but good. Jenko is always saying funny things like that.

Jenko's skin is as black as brown can be without actually *being* black. It's pretty close to actual black, though, thinks Elton. Jenko's face glows, a rosy-golden glow under the blackness, something Elton thinks of as a kind of cheer. The palms of his hands are pink, too. Elton has studied him furtively when he's peddling and Jenko is talking or checking his phone. He's handsome, Jenko. His entire body is muscular and proportioned. "Neat" is the word that comes to mind, in his bright white Nike sneakers and bright white socks, his athletic shorts and red UA T-shirt.

Elton and Jenko come from different planets.

Elton comes from the planet Xenon.

"Ah, you will find out, my friend. Oh yes. Because you will discover a woman who is made for you, and at first you might not know it is she, for she will be buried under the sand, she will be in an ugly case, do you see? But then she will open up like a beautiful flower and there it will be, the pearl, my friend, Elton. The pearl will be there for you."

"Beautiful? Sounds like a bunch of BS to me."

"Keep peddling, my friend. My Elton. Keep peddling."

"BS. It'll never happen."

"Love is like an oyster, Elton. You will find it. You will not know where it's hiding, but then suddenly, suddenly you'll feel it with your bare feet, a rough shape under the ground, and you will say to yourself, what? What's this? Pick up the ugly shell, Elton, and rinse away the seaweed and the sand and the rocks and the fish poop—"

"Fish poop," he scoffs, not laughing.

"—and like magic, you will see a bit of beautiful pink, and what?! Here it is, the inside, the true meaning of the oyster, the love, Elton, my buddy, my dear friend."

Elton shakes his head. "Can we go back to 2? I can't do this. This totally sucks."

"Elton! You only have two more minutes. Two more minutes, Elton. Stay with it, handsome friend. Can you feel it now? Can you feel your muscles building?"

Before Elton can answer, Jenko pulls his phone out of his billowy athletic shorts and studies the screen. His face widens with laughter, then he shakes his head and tucks his phone away again.

No one calls Elton. How could they? Once the doctor's assistant called him on their home phone. *This is a message for Mr. Elton Larsen.*

When they lived in Mesa, he had this friend, Laurence, who called a couple of times.

Forty-five more seconds. Forty more. Thirty. Twenty. When it's over, Jenko suggests that Elton keep on going for another minute or two—to wind down, he says. "Come on, my handsome boy. The body is an organism. Do you see? Nothing fast, nothing hurtful. You will be Arnold Schwarzenegger any day now. Bruce Willis. I can see it happening. It's like magic, my young friend. Magic, I say."

Jenko's car means a lot to him. He lucked into it, thanks to another kid on the track team whose friend needed to unload the Saturn Ion at the end of the school year and was willing to take $2,400—that was $2,000 under Blue Book value, an amazing deal for a great car! Jenko's family gives him grief about the car, because it may have been a good deal, but still, it cost *so much*—and he treats it so tenderly. Of course, they all go where he drives them, and now that his older sister Estelle has her license, she borrows it often. Well, he does keep it waxed and he changes the oil religiously, an hour's task in the alley behind their apartment building. It's not at all hard to change the oil in a car, but a lot of people in America don't do it for themselves, which still seems peculiar, an oddity that he almost admires.

When Jenko got home from his run on Sunday, Estelle was watching TV and painting her nails pink. Her two sons were at church—every Sunday, a white lady comes and takes them there, to St. Bartholomew's. It's for their spiritual education, of course, but for Estelle, the best thing about the arrangement is that it gets them out of her hair.

Jenko drank a huge amount of water, did a few final stretches, and watched the show with her. Young black Americans, dressed in a hip fashion and bright in every way, sitting around a living room and cracking each other up with their teasing. Laugh track ramping up every five or maybe ten seconds. The guy and his sister were both being set up for a blind date, which turned out to be with each other.

His love for Chrissie, a beautiful and amazing girl, a miracle girl, who actually lives in the same house as the guy who sold him the great car, is such that Jenko has infinite and complete patience with his family now, which he didn't always have before. His only disappointment is that Estelle and his mother (and, of course, also his father) don't want to hear about Chrissie and all that is beautiful about her. They are filled with their own concerns and preoccupations. When he is at home, after he has showered, when the two boys are back, when his mother returns from grocery shopping at Fry's, when his sister and his mother are making dinner, when his father is studying for his engineering test, he thinks of ways to bring her up, but they laugh at him. It isn't the same kind of laughter that he hears in response to the black family on the television, it is a laughter that says, *Look, Jenko is crazy. Look, Jenko has this and this and this, and still he wants more.*

Jenko doesn't train here; he trains at the university. Here, in the fitness facility behind the mall on Broadway, strong boys and men are everywhere, but there are also old men, and women of all ages and shapes, whom he studiously looks away from. The young men have tattoos, their heads are shaven, their T-shirts and their muscle shirts say *Hurley* or *Everlast*. They wear nice sneakers and short socks. Some look like they might be in the army, anger is in them like that. The thin ones appear to be up to something secret. Jenko made himself laugh one day, thinking maybe they're all watching romantic movies at night by themselves, crying their hearts out.

Chrissie cares for none of them. She would be unimpressed. She loves that Jenko has a dream. She loves love. She *is* love, Jenko thinks.

Now the pool, and Jenko is bouncing off the walls, bouncing on the balls of his feet, strolling up and down the length of the pool while Elton swims.

"Come on, boy, come on, handsome one," he says-sings, as the fat boy flails in the blue water, a riot in this pool frequented by smooth swimmers. Jenko likes Elton, more all the time. Right now, though, he is bored, horribly, exasperatingly bored. He wants to go think of Chrissie somewhere else, or see her—he *will* see her in two hours! But the kid is a good kid. He's a kid with troubles. He's a kid who looks at Jenko with wonder.

"Now, let's go. You have made it to five. Only one to go, and then we do backstroke."

"No!" cries Elton.

"Oh yes, little friend."

Estelle doesn't believe in love. She laughs a lot, but her laugh is not the laugh of happiness. Jenko understands why she doesn't believe in love, but he hopes that someday she will find love again. He hopes that she will find what he has found with Chrissie. His parents? Love is what they feel for their family, he knows this. Love is what they feel for him and for Estelle and for Estelle's boys, Tommy and Johnny.

When they are sitting at the table—when they were sitting at the table just last night—he brought up Chrissie, and his parents' faces did not move. Always his father's face is wide and still, and he speaks very little. He makes his presence known through a kind of terrible sonar. It is the weight of that which occurred a long time ago. Last night was no different. His mother's face also remains still. Her lovely face is ruined by her experiences in another country, another world. Even coming here, to Tucson, couldn't change that completely. Even getting an apartment at the Oasis Palms, and the gentle ministrations of the white people from the international center, and rides every Saturday to the Dairy Queen in Jenko's Saturn Ion.

Most of all, he wants peace for them, but sometimes he feels that he will not be able to share the beauty of this hope. It is like carrying something precious, he wants to tell them. I am grateful, he wants to tell them. I am grateful for this life that has brought me here, allowed us to be here, the six of us who are left. I am grateful for the feeling of driving down Speedway in my Saturn Ion with the windows down on a cool evening, my hand stretched out into the wind. I am grateful for Elton.

"You are almost done. Look at that. Look how smooth your last strokes were, hm? See how well you swim."

Elton looks up at Jenko and scowls, shakes his head. Some old ladies are swimming in the other lanes. One old lady is practically sidestroking into Elton, so he lurches closer to the edge. Elton can smell old-lady perfume or shampoo, like some kind of thick powder.

Elton's room is his castle, even if love is an oyster sometimes. Elton's room may not be an oyster, but it is purple, and it has glow-in-the-dark constellations on the ceiling. Sometimes he feels right at home there. He feels snug, like he's in a rocket ship of his own design. Sometimes though, coming home from school (hell on earth), or after going to the store, or after a neighborhood picnic, or after church, or after the family therapy session, or after the doctor's office, sometimes he feels his room isn't so much a castle or a rocket ship as a dungeon.

His mother lets him play Transformers and Iron Man. She always checks online to make sure a particular game isn't too violent. Elton doesn't worry about violence per se, because violence has never hurt him. What has hurt him is some kind of invisible thing that happens with other people out there in the world, looking in. And there is his body, his self—but can you call that, even if it is physical and hateful and vengeful, can you call that violence actually? It is soft soft soft soft soft soft, like persuasion. Like suffocation, as if his skin might turn on him, he might drown in his own flesh, one bright morning.

He has lowered himself into the hot tub now, and Jenko is stretched out on the floor nearby, comfortable as ever. Two people are in the hot tub with Elton. One of the old ladies who had been swimming, and then a middle-aged lady, like his mom. Both have their eyes closed. He imagines they've been looking and listening, and he turns from them and tries to forget they are even in this world. Jenko is on his back, checking his phone. His muscular legs are bent like grasshopper legs, his white sneakers on the cement floor surrounding the bubbling hot water. Elton sits on the top step so he doesn't get faint. Still, he loves it. He's only allowed to stay ten minutes, his mother told him.

He says, "Tell me about Chrissie again."

"It started as a regular day, a regular Tucson day with the blue sky and the sun high in the sky. I showered, so happily, so gratefully, Elton, and I dressed in clean clothes. I had to go to school to study, but first I was going to bring my second check in for the Ion. Lance said he'd be there between ten and eleven-thirty. So there I was, it was about eleven. He says just to come in, and so I knock, but then I open the door. Then—wow! Then what is happening? She is there. *She is there.* She is sitting on the couch. She's wearing a dark blue University of Arizona T-shirt and nice jeans, and she has no shoes. She's barefoot. I noticed that, Elton. You can't tell what you'll notice first, what you'll remember always. She sees me, and for a minute she just sits there, holding her textbook, and then she puts it to the side. She has dark skin for a white lady, or light skin for a black lady, I am thinking. She grew up here, I know. I can tell this, always. But mostly, I don't know anything except that her eyes are looking at me in the strangest way, the strangest and most beautiful way, Elton. As if there is something we have already shared, the two of us. Lance is talking, he's introducing us—who knows what Lance is doing! Now she gets up from the couch and I come over and we are standing near each other. We are standing near each other like two trees in a beautiful forest or two pillars holding up a famous building. And then I think, then I think—I think I am trembling then, Elton, a little bit inside. And I am so calm, too. We shake hands. It is like this, Elton, I tell you, it is like this. First, you must respect the other person. You do not have a choice in this, and it is not a terrible thing or a job. But when it comes over you, the respect is shining. Do you see? I looked into Chrissie's eyes, and she looked into mine."

He is ready, he has heard this part, and he is ready for the next part, and the heat has blossomed all around his body, as if he weighs nothing.

"Her eyes are violet, my friend, they are the color of a beautiful flower, a beautiful rose. I feel deep respect. I feel very much like getting to know this lady. I am a shy boy, Elton, like you. I am shy. But I feel inside that I must, if she will allow me, I feel I must get to know this young lady. I will ask her everything, I think to myself then. I will ask about her family, and where she grew up, and what subjects she likes in school. And so I have bravery inside now. And we stand there. We stand there and make silly conversation—both of us *flubba-flub-flub*," Jenko laughs, as he always does at this part of the story, "and yet there are her violet eyes, and the respect and the bravery, and it is now as if God himself was winking at us, the Tucson, U.S.A., sun streaming in the window, and she is there, radiant, God himself has blessed us. She came from nowhere, she came from the sea, and now she was standing before me. Just as—not Chrissie, no, not Chrissie—just as she, *your* Chrissie, will stand before you one day. One day, one day soon, my Elton, you must believe me."

Jenko is looking up at the high ceiling, smiling. The clock behind him does not work, and surrounding the pool are posters depicting beautiful people with no weight problems at all. *Could it be true? Could it be true, Jenko?*

In a moment, Elton will need to return to this world. To the two women with their eyes closed, listening. To the locker room and the one shower with a curtain, and the record book that the doctor says he has to sign: *It's more fun this way. He'll own the process, too.* They'll come back on Thursday, and then again on Saturday. He'll ask for the story again. That's what he wants, to hear the story, more than anything.

Be Who You Are

Wendy doesn't think it's right that the glove compartment should be out of bounds. Certainly, if we're going to clean a car, we really need to *clean* a car. Clean it, and, if possible, know it from the inside out: be the car.

"Out of bounds" anyway—what's his problem, saying that? Of all the people in the world, Chuck knows these things are, shall we say, flexible.

The first car of the morning is bubble-gum pink, and that's awesome, a real eye-opener. "Check it out," says Dwayne. The pink Mustang rumbles slow as it gets close to the entrance, turns, teeters forward.

"Pretty in pink," Dwayne reflects, flicking Wendy on the butt with a rag.

"That's for sure," says Wendy. At least it's different. At least it *is* different. But who's driving—an old lady? Well, appearances can be deceiving; she knows this if she knows anything.

The pink car halts smack in the middle of the car-wash esplanade, and the woman inside peers around.

"Check out the sign, Mad Maxeena," mutters Wendy.

Mad Maxeena doesn't seem to notice the ten-foot sign, *Enter Here*. Chuck's up by the welcome stand, ushering her in, leaning forward and sweeping the seven a.m. air. Finally she catches sight of him. Does she notice the *fuck you, stupid bitch* look? What he specializes in when he's not sucking up to the customers.

"The lady finds the very large door," says Dwayne. He turns to Wendy, and then just stands still and awkward, too close to her.

Dwayne is tall, his chest curved in like a spoon. He has these magnet blue eyes, blue as chrome, fierce and a little beautiful. But then he has pockmarked skin galore, and a chin that isn't quite there. It's like all his anger is in his eyes and the rest of him was just done half-assed and haphazard. He's stepping toward Wendy and she's stepping back in some kind of dance, the car-wash tango.

"Get out of my face," says Wendy. Dwayne, with his morning Gatorade. All she can see is the green rim around his mouth, and she can smell the sweet tiptoeing breath of her coworker. His anger has no follow-through. He's not her type at all.

Unless she's on Detail, which is prime, the best place to find anything is on Vacuum. Wendy and Dwayne are on Polish, but still, after the pink Mustang goes through the automatic wash, two and a half minutes of sloshing joy, the old lady loiters in the store, looking at greeting cards and air fresheners, and Wendy has her moment. Dwayne's doing windows and she's got the inside of the car.

At first it looks like old Mad Maxeena doesn't have much, just some science fiction book and a hospital bracelet hanging from her rearview mirror. She's some kind of old fucking organ donor. What you do is you lean over like you're wiping down the other door. Look past the dash, past the instrument panel and the steering wheel, into the crystal ball.

Wendy releases the glove compartment latch, lets the door fall. Just maps, receipts, a half-melted roll of duct tape, pencils with no erasers. But then: what's this? A photograph. Give it a look. It's a little girl.

It's me, Wendy thinks, holding the blue rag to her chest. She's wearing a straw hat and heart-shaped sunglasses and leaning on a tree. There are flowers. *It's me when I was a movie star. When I was a little tiny innocent girl.*

Dwayne raps on the window. *What the fuck?*

She slams the glove compartment shut and pulls herself back up, giving the wheel a last swipe. Readjusts the mirror.

"Whaddya find, sexy?" asks Dwayne, a concavity in his bright blue Wash Plus polo shirt. He's got two pairs of pants he wears to work, alternating days.

"Nothing."

"You're stealing from the old farts now, aren't you? You've got no morals at all."

"Shut the fuck up, Dwayne."

Wendy and Dwayne make $7.50 an hour. This is because they've worked at Wash Plus for over six months. You get a raise then, moving up from minimum.

"Oh shit," says Dwayne, standing by the wheel well. Here comes trouble in the form of C-H-U-C-K—Chucky Boy.

"Wendy, I need to talk to you," says Chuck. "Now. In my office."

He turns toward his truck, parked on the far side of the building.

Wendy's interior: *I was a movie star and a little girl, and I lived in a tree house. It was the kind of tree they only have in California, wispy and tall with purple flowers. Purple flowers everywhere, and when they fall, it's a snow of lavender.*

"But we're about to get hammered here," she says, her voice smaller than she intended. "Dwayne—"

"Now," Chuck says, walking. His truck is yellow with orange flames off the front wheels all the way to the back, and his rims—those rims are something else, even in Tucson. They'll murder you for your rims here. Leave you in the desert with a distinct lack of life in your body and four unadorned tires.

Wendy throws the blue rag in the barrel. She's going to miss saying "Have a nice day" to the old lady who owns the Mustang, now hobbling out to her shorn car.

"Wendy, Wendy," Chuck says after he's turned on the truck and gotten the A/C on medium and the radio on low. Chuck is thirty, twelve years older than she is. What do people do with so many years, where is it stored? Wendy can hardly imagine being that old.

Chuck's fingers don't have bones, they've got metal bars inside, same with his arms. He's part machine, like a monster from the old bag's *One Hundred Best Science Fiction Tales*. When she's with Chuck, she has two instincts at once, as if she, too, has been transformed into a mythical creature—a mermaid. Or a dodo bird.

"I've been meaning to talk to you," he says, laying his head back on the seat. "You take too long at Polish, little girl. You've got to shape up or—"

"Or what, you're going to fire me?" she says to Chuck's profile.

Actually, this is what he said *would* happen, but that was two months ago, when he first caught her stealing. Now she can see no end, no punishment, no result. Chuck calls her to the office almost every day, and she steals more and more and more.

There's a funny feeling you get from the cleansers here, a smooth-slick feeling, like your hands are made of silk and it doesn't matter where you put them any longer. There's a kind of grit the cars have, too, like sugar. Chuck puts her sugar-grit hand on his trousers.

The next car Wendy violates is some kind of boring minivan. Her hand reaches all the way under the seat, past the McDonald's toy bags and instruction sheets in eighteen languages, including legalese. She's searching for something better, for treasure. She ought to toss the bags. Vacuum should have gotten them already. But there's a clear *who-gives-a-fuck* ethos here at Wash Plus, and so sometimes, even here on Polish, there are pockets left undiscovered.

There's like twenty zillion tan minivans, and each one smells like vomit even after they squirt the juice under the seat—this time, vanilla. This particular tan minivan's got the Christian influence: a bamboo cross suctioned onto the windshield, a prayer-of-the-day book with a fake white leather cover wedged sideways into the drink holder. She finds a token to Chuck E. Cheese's—a fake coin with a fake Mickey Mouse on it with fake value but real value to someone, somewhere. Real value if you're three and it's the last coin you need to win some stupid-ass, made-in-China teddy bear. She slips it into her pocket, next to the photograph. I will use it someday, the last coin necessary. Or I'll just take the coin and throw it into the arroyo, throw it as far as I can, and it will go nowhere.

Wendy works from seven to three most days. She used to work second shift just as often, but Chuck changed her schedule. He likes her to be around when he's here, in the sunny morning.

Today—today if she gets a sign, maybe she'll quit this place.

She's had this thought before.

"My Wendy," says Dwayne to himself. My Wendy.

Chuck has separated them now. She's working the car-wash monitor, and he's still polishing away. Oh, but you're sexy in the blue shirt, even in the blue shirt, Wendy Wendy. Wasn't there some kind of fairy-tale girl called Wendy?

But I, I am just a pitiful nerd, for I bespeak not of love to those such as dear Wendy. Dwayne catches a glimpse of himself in the rearview mirror, takes a glancing assessment of his black-blue eyes, his horrid horrid skin and chin. *Skin and chin job, please*, he'd say, like the cheap bastards who rumble up and say, *I've got a coupon for the Shine 'n' Go? $4.99?* What the hell are you going to get for $4.99, dude? Meanwhile, her youth is slipping away. My stunning and royal Wendy. *The coupon actually expired two weeks ago, but can I still use it, please?*

Dwayne takes the spray cleanser and draws a big *W* on the car's interior window. A big *W*, then he fills it in with scribbles of sunlight. He's been at Wash Plus for almost ten months now, and he has systems, systems and plans and all manner of education to impart on the baby-washers, like Wendy, who started a couple months after him, and like that kid John who lasted, what, two hours? Couldn't handle Chucky Boy's attitude. You have to take it with a grain of salt or like a whole fucking cup of salt, that's what he would have told him!

Oh well. Dwayne throws the towel, drops the spray bottle back into the trench. Back in the old days, when No was working here—those were good times. No, with his weird fucking name, right? But he knew how to make the hours pass. *Game a' chance*, that's what he always said. *Game a' chance*. It was his mantra. Then No passed on to another land.

The horizon from here is a zigzag of buildings. You've got your Western Wear Outlet, your Zenith Plumbing, your Chuy's Mesquite Broiler. Then there's a layer of wires and lights. Then you've got puzzle pieces of pavement: Speedway Boulevard itself, sidewalk leading no real place. Way, way back, which you can only see if you're on Vacuum, are the mountains, the color of baby mice. That's what No said, and now every time Dwayne sees them, that's what he thinks.

Wendy, Wendy, Wendy. What if Wendy ever met his mother? He smiles when he thinks about that, a kind of skull smile. Dwayne's mother doesn't meet people well. It's not a skill she's learned in her forty years on this planet. Maybe next week—next week she'll learn about Meeting People. After that she can learn how to Have Conversations with Acquaintances, or maybe even Hold Down a Job.

"Bitch!" Chuck calls from the other side of the yard. "Rag wash. Now, yo."

Yo yourself, Chuck. Fucking Yo Yo. Yo Yo Ma.

Why is Welcome so hard for these morons, Chuck asks himself, looking on. Fucking greet the customer and sell the product. This place could be a machine, a gorgeous machine, but the concept of *greet and sell* kicks their ass every time. You've got your Honest Johns, fucking dimwits, and then you've got your BS Artists, probably the worse of the two, because they give this yellow smile and you can see the people in the cars getting all terrified and closing up to the possibility of the deal. But Chuck, who prides himself on his job, learns a little something from the dimwits and the assholes; he studies them. At the bar, he tries out Honest John, he tries out BS Artist, and then he tries something new, one of the techniques he's made up or perfected on his own. He likes the I'm Your Best Friend approach, and then there's also We're All in It Together (*Hey listen, I'll take an extra five off, just don't tell the manager*). And he likes the Practical Asshole approach (*Two days left of this sale, my man, and then not again until summer*). Summer's always around the corner, too soon, too long. It's always summer here.

He has to admit it gets old, putting on the smile when all the time you're thinking two things exactly. One: You dumb motherfucker. I'm giving you ten dollars off, is that what you actually think now? Two: You dumb motherfucker. You're not just dumb but scared now, too?

Fact of the matter is Chuck's been preoccupied lately with other developments. It was going to be the best time yet, like in the movies and everything. Just Chuck and a useless criminal in the desert and five thousand easy dollars.

He'd planned to get it on his phone camera, too. Maybe not all the action, but some stills to share.

But after what happened, certainly, his patience has waned. With the nineteen employees here at Wash Plus, with the ignorance of the owner, who rolls down from the Foothills once a week like he knows something, to empty the cash register. The employees, they're children. They need discipline; they need order. Chuck astonishes himself thinking of how little these people learned growing up. What, you never learned how to do a job well? You never learned the value of personal responsibility? Someone has to lead the blind from darkness, to get them to fucking clean a car.

So yes, lately, there is this tension. He'd call it a lack of focus on his part. Everything's balanced out like on the trunk of an elephant, and if he moves the wrong way, something's likely to—he's got more on his mind than before.

The car-wash owner has a caramel-colored Jaguar. He smokes a pipe, and so he's always got his window open just a crack. When you see him through the tinted window, it looks like he's got a helmet of gold hair and that he's on fire. The inside of the car is on fire.

"*Get over here, Dwayne*, before not after the wax dries on this Vee. You want us to lose every goddamned customer?"

He starts loud and small and ends big and in Dwayne's face and whispery hoarse, and to Dwayne, it feels like a visual/aural seesaw. But the fact is there she went again, diving down into another personal adventure. Only what the hell, that's a cop's car; Wendy, my maid, my lass, my princess, do be careful when you're expressing your inner desires in the vicinity of a brigade of Tucson police officers. I know not from personal experience, but the men in their thick polyester britches, they're rumored to be unreasonable about things like that, you know? Rifling through pads of tickets, fondling the spare .45, the keys to their catch 'em 'copter.

One last look at the lass and he's back to his job. "Don't think I don't know what you're doing with Wendy, woodchuck Chuck," Dwayne says to the hubcap of a Hummer. A nerd like me, I'm not social like this, I'm not about this, I can't compete, I'm not funny, I'm not going anyplace, I just want to make my paycheck—so just pass me by, angel of assholeness, with your damaging eyes.

"Julio, my main man," Dwayne says out loud to the Guatemalan. Everyone thinks he's Mexican, but he's not. Once he told Dwayne his family is gone. What? "I loss family," he had said. Dwayne kept that in his head for a while, through a pair of Accords, a Grand Cherokee, an Outlander. *I loss family*. It sounds, even the words for it, like an error.

It's a bitch cleaning the windows on the Humvees and the Escalades; you lean out as you lean over, try like hell not to scratch the finish with your belt or zipper. And the owners on their cell phones watch from the Guest Yard, just the other side of the sad little tip box, and most of them don't put anything in at all. Once Dwayne saw someone pretend to drop money in, a quick flip of the hand because she saw them watching. A shit-load of customers are probably doing the same, a gesture of kindness, but what you've really got is a shadow passing over the thirteen dollars that, at the end of the shift, all the workers will share. Just don't give anything, my friends. Just walk past, proudly. Hell, I'm already making $7.50 an hour.

Still, there was that one guy last week. Armless Joe, the generous wonder.

"Chuck?"

"What?" He's going through the order book, blame in his hands. "Why the hell is this detail job in this pile? Whose handwriting is this? There are no fucking initials here."

Wendy stands next to her boss, her paramour, and all around her trim little, pretty little frame she's got things hanging, things she's stolen from the cars of the day. She's got the fifty-second card in a deck, a spare key, a photograph. In the cop's sedan, she found some kind of nut or bolt, the important last part to something cops need. At the end of every shift, she's a Christmas tree.

Despite everything, though, she has walked over here to give notice, or to suggest that they date like civilized people, after hours, or even that they break off this torrid, reckless, heartbreaking affair. She hesitates, weighed down by trinkets and fear.

Here's a new car rolling into the machine. One of those squashed up girlie SUVs—a Jimmy or a CR-V. The bumper sticker says *Be Who You Are.*

"Never mind," Wendy says, and turns back toward the control center. She's got another three hours. She'll catch him later.

These men love cars. But of course: it's a car wash. As an ideal employee, you've got to have an essential passion for The Vehicle. Just like the folks at Burger King are truly gourmands at heart, and the people selling vacuum cleaners want to remake the world.

But it's different for Wendy. She's not a man, obviously. She likes to be outside, though, and this beat out the one other job she was offered: wearing a tent sign for a perpetually going out of business store, standing around like a moron for eight hours a day on Grant or Speedway. No, she didn't want that, sandwiched between plasterboards and breathing the neon lie. The worst kind of unnatural jail in the world.

Wendy folds rags. The sun has gone high and hot like a stranger tapping her shoulder. Like Dwayne, she believes people can change, that goodness will find a reward. The talent finders are out there, picking up their Starbucks and then crossing the street to Wash Plus to find her, to notice and rescue and discover.

She has to be vigilant and put all the pieces together. She has to be ready, careful, patient, prepared. Wendy is the flint of a match. Wendy is a diving board.

It's crazy odd that here comes another pink car, this one a convertible, pulling up to Welcome. No one's there, so she throws the rag and picks up a clipboard.

Methinks if you captured the dreams of me coworkers, you would have one of everything, muses Dwayne, hopping into a sedan and bringing it to the end of the line. Julio, for instance, wants to be a preacher. He told Dwayne that, and Dwayne remembers. A preacher in a car wash, now that's a laugh. The kid is from Guatemala, all right? Dwayne doesn't even know where Guatemala is, but he figures it's a hell of a spit from here, a hell of a drive in a pink car.

When Julio's not swabbing cars, he's got his arms wrapped around himself, like it's cold here, cold at a hundred degrees or more.

Dwayne thinks of his mother again, lying on the couch at home, watching her "favorite shows," which are all the shows on TV it turns out, lined up in a row. At first she liked to complain about the reality shows, but now she's on board. Now she discriminates between the good ones and the bad ones. Discrimination: always the first sign of the fall.

The apartment complex on Alvernon advertised one month free rent, but when Dwayne checked into it, they meant you had to live there first, for a year.

All the floaters, all the blue-shirted floaters. Some days they terrify Dwayne, swarming as they do, and all he wants is to scrub and clean and polish. There are the power plays, the towels tossed, the cars half finished like that other girl Maribel's tattoo. Like me own thoughts most days, he thinks, this season of woe.

Not that there aren't perks. They get half off a basic car wash, coupons that come with their paycheck, and if Dwayne had a car, he might use them, too. And there are days like this, two-pink-car days. That's worth something.

And then there's Wendy, too.

"I've got to get in the car," she says, having dispatched the pink car to Vacuum and then the automatic car wash. Next it will go to Polish.

"We all want to get in the car."

"Dwayne, Dwayne. C'mon, swap with me. Hey, I'd even kiss you if your lips weren't green."

"Methinks the girl is in love."

"You're making me laugh. Here she comes, after the SUV. It's the next one in line."

"But Chuck will have me head, Wendy."

Now she's moving in, close to his body.

"He's not watching. He doesn't see anything."

Dwayne gives up. She watches his concave self meander over to the control panel. He has wraparound mirror sunglasses that were in style about two hundred years ago, but he still has a baby cuteness to him, like some kind of sad sack loser boyfriend.

The pink car is here. The owner is a boring freak, a zombie lady. But the car! The car maintains the pleasure principle, the splash, the rub, the polish, the slide of cloth around the interior. It enlists zombies to drive it here.

Wendy lets herself in. She wipes and scans. Sometimes the glove compartment is too obvious. Plus you often don't have much time. Quickness is necessary.

She remembers the zombie's dark eyes, the question about a wax job, $29.99 too much for her.

She's got expert hands: that's what Chuck says during office hours. Now, against Wash Plus policy, she's wearing rings on five fingers. Ambassador Diamonds, a store Wendy passes in the bus every morning and every afternoon, advertises the cost of gold and silver on the marquee. Gold: $906.50 an ounce. Silver: $17.18. The rings Wendy wears on her ecstatically, otherworldly soft hands, worn smooth by the dirt of cars, worn smooth as pearls in the ocean, drift their way along the top of the upturned visor in the pink car, then between the seats, like she's copping a feel.

She's about to find something when she discovers the eyes of the car owner, staring down at her from outside. The zombie has left the greeting card selection and has come to see what Wendy is doing. The zombie is screaming.

He's trying to hear his friend give instructions, but his friend is driving— driving away fast—and the instructions come in patches. Despite his mastery of the universe, Chuck feels the sting of sweat under his arms. Feels like fire ants are biting him. "What? Sorry, you cut out there. What did you say, then?" When he's under siege, he starts talking country again, starts getting polite and confused and saying *you bet* and *what, then?* The fact is that even now, twenty years after his dad was transferred to Davis-Monthan, he still gets that balloon-about-to-pop feeling in his head from the sun. You wouldn't want to be a rodent here, in the desert. You wouldn't want to be a human being. It's a bad-luck place, with all the sand and the lizards and the scorpions crawling out of nowhere like they've been transformed from sun and sand into live things. All his luck in the world depends on if he can hear his friend's instructions. Originally they'd told him to leave the car there, with the trunk locked. Now they're telling him he has to go back, back to the location on the edge of his dreams. Go back to the car and do something. But what?

Fuck, there is no body, he wants to whine. It was a fake, an illusion. A scam. I freaked out. I'm a coward, man.

"I'm sorry, I can't hear you, what?" he says again.

Did his friend say this is only the beginning? No, he didn't say any-thing. Chuck takes the phone away from his ear and looks at it. He's dis-connected. *Welcome to AT&T Wireless*, the phone tells him.

Riddle: What's worse than being a ruthless killer?

Punch line: Not being a ruthless killer, being a no one.

He hears a scream. Someone is screaming at the polish station.

All the employees look up, a flock of blue birds. Chuck never moves fast, but right now he does seem to be barreling forward, and then here comes Dwayne, back from the bathroom where he'd been using wet paper towels to clean up the green around his mouth. Wendy is in the car. She's practi-cally lying down, relaxing.

The zombie woman holds her hands over her ears. Her hands are like mittens, and she won't stop screaming.

Wendy would like the woman to know she understands. She gets it now. She's in the embrace of the jacaranda tree, she's in the Hollywood Hills, it's springtime. She wants to tell the woman that, no, she won't take the piece of string that she's found, that she's fondling with her smooth hands. It's a six-inch piece of string, but it holds everything together. So lady, like, you can stop screaming. Take five steps back, don't step on the Windex.

I have the car keys, Wendy is thinking. The keys are in the ignition.

Chuck and Dwayne stare down at her.

"Wendy, why are you crying?" asks Dwayne.

Chuck's eyes are glazed, not understanding. In a minute he'll give the zombie, who's now moved on to some kind of low moan, two discount coupons, redeemable within two months maximum. He'll scrawl his sig-nature on the bottom line.

Dwayne wipes his chin, moist and cold. He's in love. He's in love with Wendy for sure now. For her, he'd do anything.

But Wendy is going to drive away, and she'll scatter all the things she's stolen. Out the window they'll go: a map of Texas, a girl's photograph, a token. She'll drive away, under the blue prison sky, past all the car washes in Tucson.

Orange Blossoms

Eliza is walking the interminable and daily distance between Castle Arms and CVS. Her hands stink of key, the blackened key the man gave her, the man who owns the apartment and lets her stay as long as she signs over the government checks to him in advance. "I'll do you this kindness," he said. "You may pay rent in two parts, but you'll need also to pay me twenty dollars extra, each time, for the favor." His eyebrows have not just grown together, but the hairs are like the tendrils of a plant, or the flailing arms of a drowning girl before the quicksand slips over.

It's the only key she's got, and when he first handed it to her, she looked at the black shape in her palm, a shadow of something no longer there.

She waits at the signal, and the man in the yellow vest will hold up his stop sign any minute now, and he will smile the jolly smile of the vulnerable, leading her, along with the schoolchildren, across the street and onto the other side. She hears nothing from the front of the stroller, the baby they'd given her.

Lenox Madison Ferrar III was the first name on the document. How it felt, seeing his name all spelled out like that. Until then, she hadn't been aware of the curve of the *r*'s and the *n*'s, nor the wide insistence of the three *I*'s at the end, the sense of continuity and importance that might come of him, this strange agent.

      Lenox Madison Ferrar III
      Richard M. Nutley
      John Rea
      Kyle Sorenson, Jr.

Later she saw the names a second time, in the newspaper, with small photographs of each face, ash-smooth scalps, brilliant orange around their necks, eyes and mouths and noses and cheeks scarred as if the pictures themselves had been damaged, pockmarked. For one vast moment she contemplated them, thought of what it might be like to be a mother and find your child like that, soulless in the head, willing to open up a girl like a candy bar. She already knew she was pregnant by then; the people at the building next to the courthouse had made her take a test. The nurse or whatever she was, in a green uniform with a teddy bear pin, said under her breath, "Be glad they were caught, right? That they aren't on the streets to fuck up other girls."

That night she'd lain on her bed and beat her midsection with her fists. This is what it was like: a train coming in. This is what it was like: oblivion.

Eliza stands at the threshold of CVS and the automatic door sweeps open, as if she is royalty, and lets her in.

Pushing the stroller in front of you is like pushing your face into a wall, or diving with your arms tied behind your back, or closing your eyes while driving. She herself has only driven two times. She drove her grandmother to the emergency room when she was fifteen, last year. Nanie had emphysema and she was having some kind of reaction; she couldn't breathe and she was knocking her arms against the raggedy afghan. Eliza felt she had no choice, no choice at all, but still her father was stern later. It wasn't that he didn't care about his wife's mother, but as he explained it, there was a slippery slope to everything, and you must remain vigilant. Why hadn't she called a taxi, as they'd taught her to do if she found herself in an uncomfortable situation, a situation, for instance, when an adult was belittling her family or their faith in the Lord?

Walking down the aisle, Eliza can feel the baby's face like a mask even on the other side of the stroller's blue and white checked canopy. The baby is sleeping, but she is still as massive as King Kong. At the hospital they identified her as "Baby Eliza Solvang," and two months later, the baby still does not have a name.

Anyway, she's not Baby Eliza. If she *was* Baby Eliza, Baby Eliza Solvang, then Eliza's parents would surely have come to love the little infant, just as they love her.

She goes to the back of the store and picks up what she needs—a box of Cheese Nips and some Chips Ahoy! cookies and two cans of chicken noodle soup—and she's on her way to the Coke aisle when Baby Eliza Solvang suddenly lets out a tremendous and horrible howl, like someone's twisting her leg out of joint. Eliza lets go of the stroller and rushes to the front, whispering first, "shush shush," then soon, "shut the fuck up, shut the fuck up," and she's struggling with the clasp, the two, three, eighteen clasps, and then she pulls the baby to her body and starts spinning around, the words hoarse and low in her throat, "shut the fuck up, shut the fuck up," and the baby is screaming, and when Eliza straightens her arms to get a look at the baby's face, to knock some sense into her with a look of authority, the baby is by no means looking back. The baby's face, which has some eczema, some flecks of dry and some patches where the skin is whiter and other patches where the skin is red as a candle, is all closed up, all not looking and not seeing, like

>   Lenox Madison Ferrar III
>   Richard M. Nutley
>   John Rea
>   Kyle Sorenson, Jr.,

the four of them interchangeable, their sperm swimming together in a thick sea, a cornucopia.

The thing she can't get over is the monstrous size of the child. The way she is light and small, and yet has this aura. An aura is what you'd call it, Eliza thinks, this idea a fluff, a fragment, as she humps the baby on her shoulder.

Neither father nor mother wanted to hear the details, not that she was necessarily interested in discussing them, but she couldn't help but notice the distinct lack of interest in the details on the part of these people, her parents. Indeed, when Eliza was in the hospital, it was only her mother who came to the room (her father was too upset, her mother told her), and she hugged Eliza—as best she could with Eliza's IV and the cast on her arm and the sling on her shoulder—but she didn't meet her eyes. Eliza's mother's brown bangs spanned her forehead, nearly as far as her ears, and this sharp line, slightly curled under, was all that Eliza saw. She would have done anything if her mother would only look at her, look her in the eye and tell her it would be all right, make it all right, be a mother.

Then her mother left, and Eliza turned the television back on. It was a show about Africa—poor people—children. Images of little huts,

hunched old people, and then a teenage girl. The girl was standing by herself on what looked like the edge of nowhere—three stalk trees and one
half-dead goat or deer in the background. The girl wore a scarf as clothing
and had big earrings and a nose ring, and as she talked, flies came near and
buzzed away again. The flies she ignored.

She held a baby.

Apparently the baby came after she'd been raped by a bunch of army
guys who had invaded the village.

"Janjaweed, Janjaweed," the teenage girl said. The baby was theirs—
spawn of the devil, translated the commentator. When the baby was born,
the girl's family had thrown them both out and now she was living with
her uncle, though she didn't know for how long. This was happening to
lots of girls, lots of girls who had been raped by the invading army men
from another region, another culture.

Eliza squinted at the TV, irritated. When the credits rolled by, a white-
on-black title, *The Lost Babies of Darfur*, she turned the television off.

She'd never actually heard of such a thing as this before. It was, if anything, close to what animals would do, she thought, searching for ideas.
Wild cats rejecting a kitten touched by human hands, or a mother mouse
eating her babies like little hot dogs.

It was entirely against and different from everything she'd read about
in, say, their family Bible hour, or seen on *How I Met Your Mother* for that
matter.

Eliza closed her eyes. Something like that wouldn't happen here.
Nonetheless, there was this: her father's absence, and this: the distant tiny
puppet look of her mother.

Theirs is not just a kind of Christianity, it is *the* Christian way, and it is
the way, period. And it is true that when Eliza's father spoke, after dinner,
about faith, his eyes became the softest of browns, and his hands, holding each other on the table, looked patient, kind, humble, but also strong.
Wise, strong: Daddy's hands.

Eliza remembers lying in bed together, just she and her dad, Mom
in the kitchen making breakfast. He'd read her the funnies. He read *The
Family Circus*, which had one picture only and wasn't really all that funny.
He read *Baby Blues*, also about a family, and sometimes when he read it,
she wondered, in a vague corner of her nightgowned world, why it was
"Blues"? What was blue about it, any of it, after all? He read *Marmaduke*
and *Pickles*, and he chuckled along with Eliza. And he would, at times, just

remain quiet afterward, his reading glasses in one paw, and stare out at nothing, at their feet under the covers maybe, and stroke his short beard. He was a gentle man. He always had been.

Once a week they had a family meeting. This was on Saturday, four o'clock sharp, and then they'd go out to dinner.

The last family meeting, before what happened happened, seemed typical at the beginning. The five of them—Eliza was the oldest of three— sat around the mission-style table with matching chairs that they'd gotten at American Home Furnishings with the last year's tax refund, and began, as always, with a prayer. Her father was a shorter man than some, but at this table, with these people, he was god. He had soft pale white hands, and the cuffs of his purple-green-white striped shirt were somewhat worn as he lifted his palms to the sky and began. "Our Lord in Heaven, we are your disciples. Guide us in our actions, guide us in our decisions, guide us as we try, with all our might, to live in your image, to be worthy disciples, obedient children, and humble leaders of the wicked from darkness into the light of your love." For at the Good Word Holy Family Church, where Mr. Solvang served as assistant deacon, not just *personal*, but universal, outward-reaching salvation was required. It pained him, the sinning of others.

He opened the discussion part of the meeting, inviting the others to speak first, and Sam, age five, raised his hand.

"Yes, my son?"

"Can we get the swing set now, Daddy?"

"The swing set." Mr. Solvang made a show of jotting this down.

Eleven-year-old Rachel raised her hand. "I've done the poop-scooping job for two weeks now. I think I've learned my lesson and would like to go back to my regular chores."

Mr. Solvang nodded solemnly, writing.

Neither Eliza nor her mother had anything to add that time around. Eliza's mom remained still, her eyes two amazing deep blue orbs underneath her bangs. If it weren't for the freckles and cute, baggy sweatshirts, if you just looked at her eyes, you could say to yourself: "Whoa, what planet did *she* come from?" Once, at a costume party, she wore a sequined mermaid-like bathing suit and skirt, and she wore bright green eye shadow. It wasn't that she looked beautiful, but that when she turned to Eliza after Eliza said, "Hey, Mom, where're the chips?" her eyes flashed hostile with freedom.

At the mission-style table, Mr. Solvang's own eyes were opaque, thoughtful. He dispensed with the two questions from his children—*no, yes*—and then he said that he'd had a revelation, and the revelation was that they were to move from Tucson to St. Petersburg, Florida, site of the Good Word Holy Family Church headquarters, at the end of the school year. "Father Hansen has given me his blessing. We can be an exemplary family, a showcase family, devoting our lives to the will of the Lord."

The children and the wife took in the information, and before long, the children were asking fairly predictable questions—Sam asked about Disney World and Rachel asked if her best friend could come to the beach with them—but Eliza remained silent. Her brain was funneling into a gray hole, for she was in love for the first time. Really, really in love, and she and Jon, who was Jewish, had just last week gone to third base in his mom's minivan in the school parking lot. Eliza had not gone to third, or even second base before. At this point, she didn't think anyone knew about Jon. She'd kept it quiet around the house. There was, of course, the Jewish Problem.

The feeling in her own body, this was something she'd never known before, and in their heat, it was Eliza who had pulled his hand farther down.

Baby Care 101. The hospital sent her home with a light green plastic bag, a matching bottle, a bib dotted with green bunnies, and a small towel dotted with similar animals. A plastic bag with the hospital's name on it was filled with samples of so many things: nipple ointment (disgusting thought), formula, baby powder, baby shampoo, baby moisturizer, a few diapers, a slim box of baby wipes, another package of baby wipes. Wipe, wipe, wipe. Wipe and feed and wipe and feed, but the situation is more dire than that. It's not just that the baby is monstrous in size, but every time you touch her, your hands get stuck with this invisible spider web stuff, threads of goop, and you can never get away, you can never truly get rid of it.

There is one time that Eliza likes: when the baby is sleeping in her bed. The baby lies on her side. (*Not on the stomach!* Everyone at the hospital chanted this as if that had been the cause of more death than all the wars in the universe. She knew three things for sure: *Don't put the baby on her stomach!!!!! Don't shake the baby!!!!! If you have problems with control, call this number, open twenty-four hours!!!!!*). And when little Baby Eliza Solvang was sleeping on the bed yesterday, she had her arms raised above her head, and her chin raised, and her lips were soft and parted, and it looked, for a moment, like she was having a beautiful dream of her own: a dream of bunny rabbits, a dream of a mother.

Because no matter what Eliza thinks, the baby wants her more than anything, more than life itself. *Shut the fuck up, shut the fuck up.* Eliza hears the words rehearsing, echoing, even when the tiny giant sleeps. It's at this moment when Eliza stands up, grabs her purse, and indulges in her new habit, smoking, just outside the patio door in the lascivious heat of spring—until, through the door, she hears the screaming of spider webs, and she knows the dreams are done.

Her father, soft-handed man, patient man, had the house half packed before the incident, the outrage, the concomitant punishment. Turns out he'd had a refinement of vision: instead of waiting for the school year to end, they'd simply stay through the testing season, get the kids' Stanford 9 reports, and then start homeschooling in Florida. The children had stacked plates in between sheets of newspaper. The mirrors in the house had come down and lay between towels in the master bedroom.

There's an enormity and an importance to one's place in the community, to one's role in society, to one's mission here on earth. Some are called to be leaders, to be examples for others. Some are humble and must bow to the whim of the Lord.

There's a historical, or biblical, precedent for penance. It's not that Eliza asked to be gang-raped behind Blockbuster, but she'd already been descending, and this was a wake-up call. Abortion was certainly not an option. And it wasn't like her parents had abandoned her forever; they simply required that she stay away, out of view, until the baby was older.

Why? Why couldn't she come to Florida?

Because you have failed us, Eliza. You and this child of Satan. If it hadn't been them, it would have been the Jew. Yes, we know about him.

The little baby will not stop crying, and Eliza has abandoned her basket with the Cheese Nips and the Chips Ahoy! cookies before the coolers and put the baby back in her stroller and is taking a peripheral walk around the store and back toward the front door.

This is when she runs into Jon.

When Eliza looked in the mirror this morning, this is what she saw: a grown-out haircut and bags under her eyes and a whole mess of zits on her chin, worse than she'd ever had before, and a look in her eyes that could only be described as fear. So things had gone a bit downhill since tenth grade, since she'd last seen Jon and she'd been, if not popular, at least not someone who stood out as a freak of nature.

In the meantime, Jon has gone punk. He's wearing gel in his hair.

"Eliza," Jon says, struck practically dumb. He is frozen in the middle of the automatic doors, and only jumps forward when the doors start close-opening, close-opening, in a frantic automatic half-witted hysteria.

"Jon." Eliza remembers everything: the theater of high school, the inflections, the slow turning away from the undesirable ones. She doesn't have the will to live. Here. Now. At CVS.

Jon puts a hand up to *his* chin, pitted and sore with his own furtive pickings. He lurches, like something has given way in the atmosphere. "Is this your baby?" he asks. He says it boldly, as if this is a Christmas party and she's wearing a cute pair of antlers.

"Yes." But he wouldn't go to a Christmas party. Then she thinks, of course he would. We make them go to our Christmas parties all the time.

"What's her name?" (The baby is wearing pink—maybe that's how he knew.)

Eliza thinks quickly. "Jess. Jessica."

"Wow. Holy shit, wow." Jon stands back up from where he was half-kneeling.

Eliza is rigid, hands on the stroller. She feels the roundness that has not yet left her waist, the sausage aspect. She feels the pull of the elastic band on these, not really maternity, more like XXL sweatpants she's wearing. I wouldn't be caught dead in pants like these, she's thinking. But I am caught. I am caught dead in pants like these.

"She's an okay baby," Eliza says at last. "She sleeps a lot. When she sleeps, she makes this little gurgle."

The baby, newly named, has been blessedly silent for all of this, as if the red and green Mohawk interests her.

"That's cool."

A silence, then Eliza asks, "So, how's school?"

"Sucks. You're not missing much."

They're standing in a section of firewood and clearance cosmetics, all the bottles and jars slashed and reslashed with green, then red, then yellow stickers. "Yeah," she says. "I'll probably take the GED, maybe go to college when she gets a little older."

Since when is she the concerned mother, the one with a name for her daughter, with plans for the future? The reality she's creating for Jon is disturbing, like taking off your sunglasses and blinking at a yard of scrap metal. Her headache is about to come on, but she's got a few minutes yet.

Maybe she can get the Cheese Nips and the cookies, maybe she can talk to Jon some more, or even give him her cell number—

"Well—" Jon says, the *well* that comes before departure.

The fact is, Eliza had been the one to break up with him; she'd said it would be best, that she needed to concentrate on her family now, that this was her decision, dropping out, keeping the child, breaking up with the Jewish boyfriend who had been only gentle, only sweet with her, as if all boys and reality had to be swept away in the wake of the resonant act, a funnel of time that was really only a half-hour long but was painted in darker, richer colors than other minutes, other hours.

Typically, the Christians would marry you off. Why hadn't that happened to her?

Eliza and—Jessica—trudge back to Castle Arms. Her ears are ringing. Her eyesight is going. She feels every pebble under the wheels of the stroller.

At first it's like maybe she's seeing scraps of bags or fabric remnants or balloons from a graduation party, all colors, and she thinks her headache has taken on a new dimension. But it's not that. It's a refugee family; she's seen them before. She's seen them in ones or twos, but here, there's a whole bunch together. They're on a walk on the other side of the street; they're all going to a refugee event together. Maybe they're going to refugee church. And then Eliza sees, realizes, they are all women—where are the men, the fathers and brothers?

In some of the women's arms, lashed close with batik cloth, are infants. The women lead small children in western clothing by the hand. But they, the women laughing and smiling at one another, are wearing such amazing, the most vibrant colors. One is wearing a long leaf-green and white skirt, and then wrapped around her shoulders is a purple and red shawl. One is wearing a brilliant yellow caftan and an orange turban and her dreadlocks hang out the back like tassels on a fancy curtain. Another is in red, and then there's blue, and more green, and a dark mustard yellow, and slipped inside the stretches of cloth, in the folds, every once in a while, is a small black face, like the small white face in the stroller on the other side of Fifth Street here in Tucson.

Inside her first-floor apartment, Eliza goes to the bathroom, leaving the baby in the stroller even though she has started howling. When Eliza comes back, blank yellow light comes through the shades like a malevolent life force.

It takes a while to get used to the dimness, but the drawn shades keep the heat out, at least in part. When she was pregnant, Eliza didn't think she'd breast-feed the baby, but then she was struck by the practicality of it. Wouldn't you know she'd always be losing the nipples to the bottles, or leaving the warmed-up formula in the microwave overnight? "Jessica, Jessica, Jess," Eliza says in the near dark, scrambling now to unlatch the eighteen million belts on the stroller.

A baby uses her head to express emotion, like punk rockers do. A head butt or two can mean *I'm totally pissed off.* Then they come gentler, slower, the baby turning her head this way for a second, pressing her cheek into her mother's shoulder, then turning that way, press, close eyes, brief moment of silence, while the crying jag winds itself down again. Eliza sits in the stretchy plastic chair by the dining room table. She pulls up her T-shirt and positions the baby, and Jessica begins to suck, settling down with some murmurings and grumblings into the safety and comfort here.

There is a slice of the back courtyard Eliza can see from where she's sitting: an orange tree, a section of a green garbage can, and then a flash of silver reflection that for the first couple of weeks Eliza couldn't figure out, so finally she went to investigate. It was a broken window, leaning on the wall, never picked up by the garbage collectors and never returned to someone's home, either.

At this time of year, if you keep the door open a ways, you can smell orange blossoms. It's a sweet, slow perfume, especially at night, luxurious and intoxicating as a riverboat ride or a serenade. Amazing, really, how much fragrance can come from one little tree—even if it's just for a moment before it goes away.

Jessica, she tries out, in her head. A decent name. Why didn't I think of that before?

As she sits, her head leaning on the wall, the warmth and weight of Jessica the baby melting into her, becoming her, Eliza begins to think again of the men who brought her here.

Where does religion begin? For Eliza's father, it came as a revelation at some drunken moment in an alley or someplace. Eliza has heard him talk about the *miracle of his conversion*, and she knows it involved a *last straw*, a *darkest hour*—it involved stealing from his dear aunt Josephine, taking the money she'd saved for dentures and spending it on cocaine and liquor. To illustrate his debasement, her father likes to recount that he bought silk socks, ten dollars a pair, each pair a differing hue and texture to match the pants he wore as a furniture salesman.

Pride, he calls it. One of the seven deadly sins. Eliza never did find the seven deadly sins in her Bible reading, but her father certainly was fond of the list, and later, he accused her of lust, last of the seven, and so in a sense, they were bookends. She, too, needed to hit bottom, and, though it pained him deeply, he was doing what was best for her and her child.

Eliza's new list reads something like this:

> Get diapers
> DES—bring form
> Job Bank Saturday
> Call about GED practice test schedule
> Lightbulbs
> Talk to landlord about sink

Her father cried when he told her about his pain and her release. She'd seen him cry before, during Mass, but here he was crying in their kitchen. Tears ran from behind his glasses down into his beard. He held his hands out, somewhere between him and her, wavering. Palms up, palms soft and white as clouds. It was as if those hands were melting, becoming unformed, turning back to God, turning into light, into butter, there in the kitchen, before he himself turned from her.

In a sense, she felt like she had a revelation at that moment. Eliza's body was still stressed from *the ordeal*, as her mother called it; she had gray patches like clouds around her thighs and calves. Her insides had swollen and the two sides chafed when she walked, like she was holding a prickly pillow between her legs. The back of her head was scraped clean, she'd lost hunks of hair, and her skin was still pink and hairless and prickled with red dots in places: neck, cheeks, wrists. They were like stigmata, these places of pain, and yet she felt faith rush from her.

Still, she cannot languish here, in faithlessness, forever.

When she thinks of her mother now, it's as if she's looking into a camera and the telephoto lens is drawing in, sucking back in, and all things are getting small and distant. Her mother's absence is loud and red, but her image is there, tiny, like a little doll in a balsa-wood house in the corner.

Eliza flips the baby around to the other breast, gently, because that is how she has learned to keep the child quiet. Besides, this is what you do with a gentle quiet fragile thing, you act gentle quiet fragile, too, you whisper and tiptoe and make smooth sounds. You do this as much as you can, plowing over the *shut the fuck ups* that come out of nowhere.

What can a baby remember? The baby seems forgiving, thinks Eliza. If I hold her all day and night, if we are joined together, the same person, even that would not be too much for her.

My own father—but she does not go there. It's funny to think that the men, the defendants,

> Lenox Madison Ferrar III
> Richard M. Nutley
> John Rea
> Kyle Sorenson, Jr.,

mean so little to her.

The doorbell rings, slapping Eliza out of a slumber. She starts, almost waking the baby in her arms. Eliza's headache settles in as she tries to focus, tries to imagine whom it could be. The landlord is the only person who ever comes here.

The bell rings again. Eliza stands, puts the sleeping baby back into the stroller and walks toward the front door. Through the plastic edges, she sees a wavy shape of color. She opens the door; one of the African refugee women is standing there.

At first, Eliza cannot understand what she is saying, and then finally she realizes the woman is telling her that today is International Women's Day, and that here is a flyer about a festival at Himmel Park. Many women will be there, many many, and they will be selling bracelets and necklaces and rings made of leather.

"Why did you come here?" is all Eliza can think to say.

The woman on her doorstep has a small, etched face. Her neck is thin, and as she speaks, Eliza notices the tendons tense and thrum in a fearful way. She doesn't know much English, so the message about International Women's Day and the festival at the park comes in multiple throws, repetitions, returns, and Eliza understands finally but does not understand the one thing: *why here, why her?*

"Do you have a baby, too?" Eliza asks.

"I have a baby boy. He is with my mother now, but he will be at the festival. You can meet him, his name is Faisal."

"Faisal?"

The woman's hands, strong and thin like her neck, are wrapped around the neon pink flyers.

Eliza looks back at the woman, this stranger. She hesitates, but then she says, "My baby is named Jessica."

Late Night on the Radio

Do you know what happened at my son's school today? Today at my son's school, they took away all the old crappy textbooks and replaced them with the most beautiful textbooks you've ever seen in the world. These beautiful textbooks have sleek neon covers, and they're snaked around the edges with flashing red and blue lights, a coil of flash, attracting and distracting, but first of all attracting, the students, the children—our children. These textbooks are placements, my friends, corporate placements, sold to the schools for dual, or let's make that triple, purposes. You've got your discount textbook sales, awesome, all the willing, economizing high schools across the country. That's just the beginning; that's chump change. Here we go. What do you come to first, in this school textbook, this so-called book of history? First thing you come to is a fat section of coupons. Twenty pages of color coupons, page after page of coupons from fudge-creekery Burger King and Taco John's. Free burgers, free French fries, free MP3s. *Burger King.* All right, bad enough, a real problem, but then you have—content. Prime objective, my friends. What, pray, is inside *Our America: Then and Now*? Well, listen. Listen to me. I spent most of today, this whole afternoon and evening reading this, this—going beyond the flashing lights and the coupons. I guess you have to ask yourself, who's written these new pages? Whose language is this? Case in point. It's *urgent*, people. It's really urgent is what I'm saying. And I quote:

> *Arizona has been under siege for some decades. A monument to the achievements of frontiersmen and freethinkers, in recent years the state has been shackled by the federal government and its anti-freedom regulations and directives. Nonetheless, the former Confederate Territory*

> *of Arizona has taken measure of its adversaries and is,*
> *in recent times, systematizing its own survival, thanks in*
> *no small part to its citizens' ingenuity, patriotism, and*
> *strength of character.*

That's from page sixty-seven, in the Wild West section.

Dear, dear friends out there in the black night. This is a history book written by a company you've never heard of, sponsored by corporations with no altruism, no intellectual insight. This is the history book that my son, age fifteen, is reading. When he is not being distracted by the neon lights and the free triple-sized macho fries. But no, that's not Jimmy. My son is smart, he's pretty quick, and he could tell something was wrong with this picture. He brought this to my attention—*Dad, what's up with this?* So thanks, Jimmy. But not everyone can be like that—brought up to doubt and question. We have to look out for each other.

Let me give you a second example. My neighbor, we've been living on the same street for twenty years, she teaches English. Her name is Sonya. She teaches sophomores and juniors in one of our high schools— I'm going to keep the name of the school out of this right now. She's out there every day, fighting like you wouldn't believe, trying to help kids see themselves in literature, to see *others* in literature. All right, let me tell you this, see if you can believe this. My friend Sonya had to teach her class in the hall for six months last year—she was teaching in *the hall*. Monday through Friday it's like this for Sonya, and sometimes she's tapped out, yes—she's tired—but she's also tapped *into*. Compare it to drinking tequila and coffee at the same time. Or walking a tightrope. Do you think next time she'll have to teach on the roof? Maybe teach with her hands tied behind her back, or maybe with a gag in her mouth? How about if she has to teach from jail?

[Dead air.]

She assigned . . . she's always assigning challenging work. She assigned Ntozake Shange, she assigned Samuel Beckett, too. The tenth graders were waiting for Godot in her class. They were trying to decide if the rainbow is enough. Sonya is passionate, is what I'm trying to say. She loves it. She loves teaching. She loves theater.

The point is she never gives up on people. *Make do with less, make do with less,* that's the situation here, every year less, every month less, every week. Yes, it gets her down. She's only human. But Jesus, Mary, and Joseph—she's the epitome of a good teacher, a real teacher. And you want to know where she is now? Sonya? Exactly? She's in jail. Sonya is in jail because someone, someone in the fudge-creekery administration, got his hands on her reading list, and he objected to it in toto. In particular, he objected to Shange—he couldn't make heads or tails of Beckett, so he couldn't object to that—and he objected to Alberto Ríos, too. Give me a break, people. Alberto Ríos—his poetry is wholesome, if you want to know the truth. It's family values up the wazoo. It's fudge-creekery wholesome, my friends. Our man Ríos, from Nogales, dear listeners. But no Ríos and no Shange for our children, no Sonya for our students, because she, brave Sonya, defied the wicked administrator and the State of Arizona and now she is paying for it.

Meanwhile my son, your son, your daughter—will be cutting coupons for burgers. They'll be scratching their heads at the absences, at the untruths in the textbooks.

Do you know how hard it is to ferret out the particulars of history when you're fifteen, and all is fudge-creekery around you, and your guides simply want to anesthetize you, take down any instigator of thought in your world?

[Dead air.]

We're going to go back to the music in a minute. But I do wonder, at what actual point do we become afraid? Where are we in this plow-over of history?

[Dead air.]

I'm watering Sonya's plants on her front porch while she's away. While she's incarcerated, which will probably be a couple of weeks, or months. Or longer—I don't know how long. The fact of the matter is I don't know how long it will be.

[Dead air.]

Her sister has taken her cat, so that's good.

[Dead air.]

Are you listening? Is anyone listening?

[Dead air.]

I'll be watering these plants, thinking of you, Sonya.

We're going to return to the music now, with Los Papines, a track from *Here Comes El Son: Songs of the Beatles with a Cuban Twist*, a great compilation that came out, oh, way back in 2000. All right, here it is, here's "Hello, Goodbye."

Enjoy.

ESCAPE

The Lotus Eaters

Artesia jumped the fence into the broken-down-to-crap miniature golf course, and then came Pog, and then Paul and the other girl. The world was a gorgeous chocolate brown, a gleaming purring soft color that also glittered. Artesia was one of a kind, she was safe, and she had the power.

It was more of a lurch than a jump, and when her jeans got stuck on a wire, she did plunge for a second, experiencing a lightning bolt of insecurity, not enough to really throw her. She hit the ground and then she was on her feet again, the earth a trampoline. Big grin. Her heart pulsed, throbbing with the brown-red core of sheer and perfect life, and there was more to this night than they knew, than anyone could know. This night would last forever, this night was a place you could curl up into and doze, never go home, this night *was* home. For Artesia. For Artesia and Paul. For Pog and the other girl, too, probably, maybe.

This is the magic world where the ages of time abide in a garden of serenity with perpetual peace and harmony.

"Look!" she shouted, pointing at the sign near the dead building. The miniature golf course was an endless universe, about the size of a Walgreens parking lot. A car dealership now owned the property. Six months ago, the golf course had gone out of business, and the retro-tacky-trashy-mystifying world within a world began to disintegrate. Currently in a state of high demolishment, by vandals or design, the course still held on to its dismal charm. Artesia and Paul and Pog and the other girl, they'd needed something—a culminating event—after Bookman's kicked them out. And so they pranced across the parking lot and across Speedway, past the golf course's entrance and to the back of the lot, where no one could see them lurking and jumping. Now they were in, and it *was* an enchanted kingdom, all right. Punitive lights from passing cars rushed over them and disappeared again.

Paul and the rest right behind her—all too fucking funny for words. The funny genie sat on his ass on top of the banner, *Magic Carpet Golf,* the name unfurling radiantly underneath him. Used to be lit up, the man on his carpet, and now his smile alone kept him sane.

"I used to come here as a kid!" Artesia screamed.

"Shut the fuck up!" everyone said.

"Oh shit, I used to come here on my birthday!"

"So did I, who gives a shit!" Pog screamed back. He had turned away, morphing into a Black Shape—yes, all you could see was his fat black back like he was some kind of mammoth. Poor sweet Pog, forever the younger brother of yesterday's dealer. You couldn't even see his head behind his shoulders, and when you did, it looked like a tiny pinhead. He was foraging around in the corners. What the fuck was he doing? He was foraging. Along the edge in the wild zone, looking for something.

"You look like the—the—" Artesia said, or tried to say.

The moon was square, a hunk of light someone had thrown into the sky, as if the world itself weren't yet complete. It was a rough draft, gonna get the details right later. And here we are, thought Artesia. Amazing. The word *amazing* being an embodiment, or a full-on true reality.

Artesia was gritting the crap out of her teeth.

"Here is an arrow," intoned the other girl, pointing at a small sign. *Bitch. Slut.*

But Artesia so didn't totally care about that. It was all right, because . . .

"You look like, like the—"

Then here came Paul—the *god of light!*—charging up the path from wherever he'd gone, and he had some kind of long device, a crop or a wand, and as he ran, he was elegant and handsome and sexy, as always, as before, and he was hitting whatever the hell was still standing up in this place. Sexy, yes, but sex didn't come into it here. The adventure was complete just as it was, not so partitioned off as sex. Sex was—it wasn't something to look at now. It could be there, in a box, but. . . . You could have sex, but it would be some other time, the perfect time, and this wasn't the perfect time yet. Besides, there was the possibility that some realities, scrawny as they were, from the world outside the fence, could also exist here, infinitesimally, reminders, or barriers perhaps? No, *not,* and she was no longer thinking that way.

"We should go where the arrow points," the other girl said. Her legs were bowed, jeans tight around her belly and hips. She was younger than the rest of them, probably fifteen. On her own, she'd said, parents—*poof*—magically disappeared. From here, all Artesia could see was lumpy skin squeezing out from above her jeans, the girl's long hair, and her arm pointing to the red arrow painted on the broken-up sidewalk. Suddenly Artesia moved. She didn't want to be behind them anymore.

"Yes!" Paul said, his voice luxurious. "C'mon, Pog, let's go. Artesia, come on, baby gorgeous." Giving Artesia the most intense sun-god smile, a full century's worth of love and truth in that smile, in what they had once shared. The other girl looked up from the painted arrow and smiled at him then, too. He smiled back. A lesser smile.

"You look like the fucking *Hunchback of Notre Dame!*" Artesia screamed, totally remembering. But the moment had passed, and Pog was far ahead, and they were all four running again, running like wonderful wild animals, animals of the forest, and here was the path; they could smell the night. They were hidden from cars and cops and the outside world. They were safe.

Run they did, and in the half-drafted moon's light, they saw the skeleton trace of paths through the golf course. The paths, all crumbling cement, were reminiscent of the octopus hole (Hole #8). "I remember the octopus," Artesia said or thought or shouted. He was bigheaded and silver, with strangling long arms that went everywhere, this fat-ass head . . . the paths were like him, or like a skeleton. Follow the crumbling paths. Artesia took uptight piano-teacher chipmunk steps up three stairs covered with wrecked carpet. And then the path just ended. All alone on the little lift, Artesia. The scraggly old palms, thin and a billion feet high with like a powder puff up top and no coconuts, "No coconuts," she was mumbling, and then the wrecked, ugly, dried-out bushes and some grasses—the monsoon had been a fucking nothing this year, and everything was dead dead dead dead dead dead dead, and it was still actually *hot*, at midnight, a beautiful hot now, gorgeous brown mahogany everything she saw—*baby gorgeous*, he'd said—and it was like velvet, and there was truth here. "It's all around us," she was saying, the skeleton path and the funny stairs to nothing, a hangman's last stand, and if you squinted, you could see the pieces of bunched-up old bits of green, what passed for a lawn or grass, even in the glorious old days—"The past," she said, "Birthdays," and they were still near, her *friends*, and she turned around and screamed "*Path to nowhere!*" and the other girl screamed "*Shut the fuck up!*" and they were all laughing and stumbling up the cement path, to the left now, under the blasted last bit of a monkey's tail, the biggest monkey looking for coconuts.

Now here was the sphinx, rising out of the dark, a beautiful sedate god. They stood and stared. Behind the sphinx hung the moon (real, in the sky), and this was where the funny little sun king used to be, a sweet sun face smiling like a flower more than the sun, sweeter than the sun. And inside the sphinx was a bench. She remembered the cool feeling in the middle of summer, on her birthday, remembered waiting for the others, remembered that there were bees, remembered the color of her ball.

"Here you are," said Paul.

"My God," said Pog, "my God!"

"I love the world," said the girl.

Paul who didn't go to college anymore. Artesia who didn't live at home anymore. Paul and Artesia who didn't work at Ghost Fish Grill anymore—well, Paul did, he'd come back as a sub, but Artesia got her ass fired, manager wouldn't tell her why, probably because he was a fucking racist. Fired both her and Nico, and Nico was now who knows where? He was too old for the fun to be had in Tucson. When Artesia realized how much fun there was to be had here, how there was this whole different, as they call it, *safety net*, she just did it, the other thing, the *trust exercise*. She put her arms out and fell back into the city's arms.

Her mother: *what a fucking bitch!*

But she loved her mother, Artesia somehow articulated to herself. There was room for loving her mother, room for loving this fat slut girl, too—shit, she didn't know better. She couldn't help that boys thought it was fucking cute to be clueless like that. Artesia loved everyone, the world was hers, the Magic Carpet Golf Course was the universe as she knew it. And like he was reading her mind, "It's a magic carpet," said Pog, looking with wonder at his feet, and then stepping forward, falling forward, *one, two, one, two,* now not so much the *fucking Hunchback of Notre Dame!* as the Abominable Snowman. Big Foot. She was going to say it but then couldn't—her throat was hollow, a hole, she was shuddering with sensitivity, a fragment of a cloud had trailed over the moon. But the sphinx was secure—and so they all followed Pog up into the body of the golden sphinx, a cave of knowledge and power.

Paul grabbed her leg and then her ass and then her leg again as they stumbled up the hill. Artesia was laughing. All was as it should be, part of a larger order. But there was something else, too. She felt it in the back of her throat. What had seemed like hollowness was actually a spasm of nausea, and she tasted puke as she swallowed down.

They sat hunched together in the dark, and they hugged, everyone's arms around everyone else, and Paul said, "Let the sphinx be with us," and they bowed their heads and prayed. They were freezing now with fear because it was true that spirits existed; the world was not just what we saw but what we felt. What we felt *was* invisible, but it existed, did it not? Children knew this—just look at them with their Ouija boards. And look at prayers of all kinds. Look around at what made things real. Invisible things made us who we were.

"I used to come here for birthday parties," Artesia said again. Her mother held the scorecard and wore a straw hat and a dress. She had woven green ribbon into baskets and put packets of sunflower seeds and tiny spades and gardening gloves into each one and gave them to each guest, and they also had a tea party. Her mother was married to her father then. They owned a reddish-brown dog named Valentine. At the birthday party, everyone was laughing. No one minded the bees in the sphinx, coming out of the sphinx and coming right at them. No, wait. It wasn't her mother who had woven ribbon into the baskets. That was Alicia's mother, that one time.

"Why are you shivering?" Paul's voice, very near.

"I was thinking of my birthday party."

"What?" said Pog. "Not that shit again."

"Don't worry," said Paul.

"But why not?" In the belly of the sphinx, it was possible he knew everything.

"It's all an illusion," he said.

Other Girl was giggling, and they were all having trouble holding onto their cigarettes; it was hard to tell if they'd just lit them, or if they *were* lit, or if it was time to have another one.

"Look," said Pog.

Crazy ghosts stood or flew on the other side of the sphinx. On the other side of the sun that wasn't there and the moon that was.

"Oh shit," said Artesia. They ran over to the ghosts. Ten feet tall, two of them. Pure moon-stunned white with birth-defect flipper arms, like they weren't ghosts but dancing porpoises with black alien eyes. It was possible they were beneficent creatures, beneficent but so very sad, as if they'd seen something they didn't understand. As if they were trying to dance on a pretty little planet in the middle of a nuclear war.

Pog was crying.

★

Long earlobes denote aristocratic birth. Mark on forehead is symbol of spiri-
tual insight, said the sign in front of the big blue Buddha, another chicken
wire and cement god, fat brother to the sphinx. The sleeper child. The
four runners passed by, laughing. There was a magic fish and an ostrich,
and inside Artesia the memory of that ostrich's mean beak coming down
on her pink golf ball and destroying her chances for an eight on #11. Paul
said, "Touch and have plenty, touch and be lucky," as they passed the fish,
and they all put their hands on the fish's scales, and then the other girl had
the idea of getting into the belly of the fish. "Come out, lucky child," said
Paul. "Come out," said Pog. Artesia stared at the palm treetops, at a flash
of what seemed like blue light, no coconuts. Palms = prison bars. Paul
was in the lucky fish, kissing the other girl. Did that happen? Was that
happening? Now they were running back down the paths that spread like
an octopus.

Jumping over emptiness, avoiding the black lake of night and the
broken glass and the crushed concrete, Artesia fell on a piece of rebar and
ripped open her arm. Under the tiki head, Paul held her hand, licking the
wet skin. She was crying with happiness. "The tiki man has lost his head,"
she said again and again. There used to be a lookout at the top, but her
mom wouldn't let her go up there. The tiki man's face was long and lean
and giant and sad. "Do you understand? I love you," Paul said, kissing
her arm, the gash from the rebar throbbing like the Holy Ghost, like the
Sacred Heart. Artesia, laughing. "There was the red ant hole and that was
funny and the alligator you hit the ball right into him and there was the
monkey, too, but most of all I liked to go on the blue boat, the beautiful
blue boat, and my mother would wear these dresses like from the fifties,
but now we don't even talk. She called the cops on me and threw my shit
outside. She threw my clock radio outside and my shoes. There was the
funny red bull with his sad eyes, and a scary skull and the rattlesnake den
more like a big dirt heap than any kind of real snake place." But Artesia
wasn't actually speaking. *"You slut! You slut!"* screamed the other girl, right
up in her face. *"He's my boyfriend!"* Now the other girl was crying and Pog
was saying, "Let's go," and Paul's smile was aimed right between the other
girl and Artesia, as if he were an architect who knew the exact middle of
things, a physicist who knew the exact middle of things. The way he'd
pushed her against the wall of the empty pool and the way he'd held her
hands. The way they loved and knew everything like psychic people in

the night. She'd tried to act big, mature, after the restaurant. Before her mother gave Snickers to the Humane Society and threw her shoes in the alley and when she and her sister Chelsea—it had all been so long ago, and now she was out here, in the good city. Adventure was to be had. She knew, she'd always known, more than him. College boy. But still, he had something, a golden charm, a radiating essential thing that only she understood. The brown velvet of the night was fading, and the tiki head had taken on a gray cast. The stalky plants were looking less enchanted and more like something that would be razed soon, forgotten along with all the monkeys and flowers and aliens.

Pog and Paul and the other girl were lying in the bottom of the blue boat, holding hands. Artesia stood on the bow, and it was only then that a few drops of rain came. The stringy cloud had thickened and diffused. "We can't stay here," she said. Paul's hand had disappeared up the other girl's shirt, and Pog was holding her legs. One gangplank went into the blue boat, and another went out. You could come and go like that. The girl was laughing; they were all laughing. Artesia held herself in her arms and stood alone, the figurehead on a ship, face turned.

The Three Graces

Alyssa's long black hair shines as in the Pantene advertisement, a river of black, so lush it's almost frightening. She wears it pulled back from her face with a pink band. She is wearing massive stud earrings that Sarah and Terri pray are cubic zirconia, though they can't be sure, what with Alyssa's lover's penchant for spoiling. They've heard he's wealthier than Croesus—this aspect of his person overshadowing all others (overshadowing, for instance, Alyssa's assertion that he is funny and smart and can give her an orgasm with stealth, surgical precision). Alyssa is peering at a potted barrel cactus. She's half crocked, or so it would seem from the way she's weaving.

Sarah would hate to think that. She'd hate to think Alyssa was drinking alone—maybe in the ladies' room? Or before they even convened this Sunday afternoon?

The barrel cactus is beautiful. The yellow spikes all bend slightly, symmetrical rows of brilliant yellow stars against the meat of the cactus, itself a lurid, sinister green. All in all, the tableau—Alyssa's hair, Alyssa's jewels, Alyssa's pink hair band, and then the bright spikes and the green barrel and the blue sky beyond—is really quite striking, and just now inducing a migraine in Sarah as she stands near a tall, hallucinogen-producing cactus with a name she can't think of right now. This one looks like something's been gnawing at it. Some drug-addled blackbird is zigzagging through Nature now, its doomed eggs in the stash house. Or maybe the puckered holes were made by a rat, a desert rat (like her ex, Wilbur!), or some ominous, way-oversize flying insect, a tarantula hawk or kissing bug (it sucks your blood—another great fucking reminder). Sarah is more or less grimacing now, despite the brilliance of the scene and her usual disposition. In a minute, she'll rearrange her face to look cheerful.

"Oh shit, these are gorgeous," says Terri, Sarah's sister from Phoenix (recently moved from the East Coast). "And they're so *cheap*. I wish I didn't have the sedan or I'd take some back with me. Can you keep them in the car all day, anyway? Can cactuses—or what the fuck, you call them *cacti*, Sarah, right? Cacti, cacti. Can they get heatstroke and die?"

"I love it," says Alyssa, still dreamily staring at the barrel cactus and looking beautiful with her exceptional chin. Her chin and jaw—they go in, Sarah doesn't know, four inches or something. Yet her chin doesn't *jut*. She has a thin neck, too, and overall a ridiculously distinguished beauty, as if she's from Europe or some other place of ancestral elegance. She's the type who can wear just a T-shirt and look good, further considers Sarah, though the thought goes more like this: *Gorgeous. Damn fucking T shirt.* Her headache preventing complete sentences.

The three women are at the Members' Preview Plant Sale at Tohono Chul Park. Sarah is the one with the membership, and so she brought her sister and her neighbor, Alyssa. Sarah and Alyssa's friendship sprouts up in brief, tranquil no-expectations ways, only to wither and then later to return again. They've known each other for three years. They both enjoy gardening, and sometimes shop for clothes (Alyssa has more money than Sarah, but she claims to relish the deals at Buffalo Exchange or Ross Dress for Less—"You can really get some great stuff!"), or for fresh vegetables and fruit at the farmers' market on Saturdays. They both shop at Whole Foods, although never together. Sarah also frequents Trader Joe's.

Five years younger. Maybe six.

Alyssa lowers herself in a kind of ballerina's squat, wrapping her arms clear around the barrel cactus's pot, and then slowly and, without so much as a wobble, rises up, her smooth skin disconcertingly close to the unforgiving yellow needles.

"I'm taking this one. I'm in love," says Alyssa. She smiles at Sarah first, and keeps the smile on for Sarah's sister.

"That's great!" says Terri, who *is* actually drunk today, on sadness. She lost her dog, Fandango, two days ago. The red dachshund was poisoned, and she had to make the final call to have him put down. The next day she drove one hundred miles down from Phoenix to be with her sister, actually her twin. (Twins, but that doesn't mean they're preternaturally or mystically bonded. And this doesn't have anything to do with the fact that they're *fraternal* twins, either, the dissing of their subset being incredibly annoying to Sarah—as if distinction itself were a flaw.)

Tucsonans might trash their sister city, but all things considered, Phoenix does wield some charms. It has an echelon of restaurants and hotels mostly lacking here, for instance. Because landowners care not about the cost of water or the environmental impact of watering the desert, it's much greener overall. Little rivulets by malls. Major, awesome lawns. In fact, it was some kind of hardcore lawn fertilizer that killed Fandango . . . at this moment being cremated. Or who will be, soon. His body is waiting somewhere, in the sort of place it's preferable not to think about at all.

All beauty is wasted, all beauty will end, Terri is thinking, keenly aware of the unholy joke of immediate, rude extinction, the disregard the majority partner seems to have when it comes to maintaining the social contract— the capacity *to be* social, as Terri now interprets it, to look and listen and feel. *Fandango is dead.* And it goes on from there: we're talking doom, individually and in great swaths. We're talking the aging process. And so you need to capture life for the brief moments you can. Look at that barrel cactus.

Terri would not have come down to Tucson if Chris had been around, but he is working on a project in New Orleans this week. The kids are also both gone for the night—sleepovers. To be frank, her husband may not have been as helpful as Sarah (a good listener, Terri knows), because he adopts a fatalistic, purportedly practical stance in times of trouble: "It was his time," "Crying can't bring him back," "We'll get another one," et cetera. Still, it would have felt awkward to leave for the weekend, if he were home. "Sisters have a special bond" might have come in handy in that circumstance. All in all, it was cleaner and easier not to have had to talk about it, to have just gotten in the car, turned on the A/C, and pretended for a couple of hours that life could be a song on the radio and a Starbucks in the cup holder and vague attention to a stretch of highway notable for its ugliness, give or take a few patches of cacti, a kitschy ostrich farm, and Picacho Peak, a lump of molten lava people climb when they have nothing better to do.

Poor Sarah. She looks like complete shit. Her very thinness looks unhealthy, a diminishing. Not the product of a compulsive fitness regimen, but of illness and overwork. It's all because of that moron Wilbur. Ever since he broke up with her, Sarah has been a tall, thin moper. She looks like an ostrich herself, hanging her head.

"To hell with it," says Terri, "I'm going to buy one of these small ones and just see how it does in the car."

"Good," says Sarah.

"I know, you have to, right?" says Alyssa.

And so the three women trudge farther into the maelstrom of xeriscape terrain, pots filled with this and that Martian-like form: the one with glorious black hair holding the spiky thing to her belly as if she's pregnant; the squat, shorter one from Phoenix holding up, as if for inspection, a fat miniature cactus with a pink head, resembling the penis of a prickly circumcised frontiersman; the willowy one with the membership card and the 20 percent discount not holding anything at all but casting the remnant of her gaze bitterly over the entire venue, or so it seems.

The cacti aren't really dry or barren. They just know how to conserve.

"Oh fuck," says Alyssa, halting in her tracks.

"What?" say the others, nearly trundling into her pretty back. The gravel crunches loudly—Terri's modest sandals and Sarah's Nike trainers.

There's Zero and his wife, looking at one of two mature saguaros for sale.

Zero's wife's hair is also magnificent—of the three women, only Alyssa immediately knows its a wig. It's a ginger color not often found in nature, cut in a perfectly symmetrical bob. Hanna Daitch puts her hands up to the strands surrounding her face and pushes back. The gesture is tentative, almost shy, as if she's never done it before, a man pretending to be a lady. But she's not pretending to be who she is, because men almost never get breast cancer. They don't get double mastectomies up in Phoenix while their sweet, sexy, rich husbands mourn back in Tucson in the languorous arms of their black-haired Other Woman. And for all Alyssa's surface ease and confidence, for all her insouciance and demand for frankness that Zero thinks of as ethnic somehow—Latin—Alyssa is momentarily stunned speechless. She doesn't know what to do next.

With a migraine sufferer's instinct for sizing up a situation (some would call it clairvoyance), Sarah knows immediately who they're looking at, and her eyes drift from the handsome, well-dressed, fifty-something woman (Sigrid Olsen vest with red beading and lace fringe, pinstripe capris, espadrilles, a silk-screen top apparently depicting French signage and graffiti overlaying sections of Toulouse-Lautrec's more lurid bar scenes, gleaming thick-stemmed sunglasses, downturned face), and looks at Zero himself, bigwig at Raytheon. Why, he looks like a little pig. A hairy little pig—a javelina for fuck's sake—not some stealth orgasm-giver! He's— he's probably five feet tall and his feet are stubby and fat, ballooning out of two-tone Bally loafers (Sarah and Terri's dad's favorite, the only brand of shoes he ever bought, actually). He's wearing white socks and what Sarah imagines are some kind of tennis shorts, hitting midthigh at best, a length in fashion back when Björn Borg was playing. And perhaps Piggy Stealth Orgasm Giver would have been young enough to wear such shorts in '78, too, thinks Sarah, indulging in gleeful horror as she takes in the physical presence of this man about whom she's heard great things. Great things.

Alyssa has frozen up entirely. It's only Terri who doesn't know what's going on, not in the slightest, though earlier she did hear Sarah and Alyssa talk briefly about Alyssa's "special friend," and she saw her sister mutter the way she does when she's feeling peevish—which is often! But Terri understands that Sarah is, let's face it, just miserable about how things are going, love life–wise. She's living the nightmare in which she is over thirty and marriage is but a mirage on the horizon, always receding, and she's growing desperate and kind in ways people oughtn't to be—kind to jerks and assholes—and increasingly devoted to her cat, Lala, a dust bunny with bones inside. Terri understands, *of course* she understands, the devotion! It's just that poor Sarah has lost sight—not of the important things, because Lala *is* important, but of the impression, say, she makes on others. She's lived alone too long. She's becoming a hysterical eccentric who drinks herbal tea and prefers mauve to every other color and is prone to fetishistic spurts of devotion to spiritual gurus she's read about online. And who *could* really get excited about that job of hers, anyway? Sarah isn't really interested in grant writing. She'd rather be gardening, or going to massage school, or working in sports—Sarah likes sports! What the hell is she *doing*, wasting her life like this with the dreariest of office/academia jobs imaginable? How has it come to this? Still, she is Sarah, good, listening Sarah, smart Sarah, Sarah whom Terri adores. . . .

But through the fugue state of grief and complacency in her own Functioning Marriage (twelve years and counting! Kids in middle school! No broken bones, no affairs, just a prolonged status quo like an oil painting of a lake with a lily pad or two, surrounded by pine trees, a little duck in front, waddling—and in this landscape, she wears a cape, a cape of superness, she is a suburban superhero!), Terri, holding her baby cactus, is suddenly aware that the two well-appointed people on the path in front of them are staring at Alyssa, Sarah, and herself, and that Alyssa is now turning hastily, knocking into Sarah, who knocks into Terri, and the big and the small cacti both make contact with human skin, causing tiny piercing wounds in all three women somehow. Then in a cursing, disorganized jumble, variously bleeding, Alyssa, Sarah, and Terri turn back to look again at the well-appointed people standing stock-still, the power of their stares now taking on telekinetic force field proportions. That man is wearing Dad's shoes, Terri thinks dimly.

The woman, though, with the ginger bob. Her face has gone chalky. Slowly she takes off her sunglasses. Her eyes are filled with the kind of pain and sorrow usually seen in paintings of saints or martyrs. As if they are a living force, the pain and sorrow begin to change—change her! She's expanding, becoming huge, right in front of them on the path. Her head is as big as a car tire, her expression a supernatural embodiment of anger. Terri is frightened, because she feels that she might not have been paying attention—that something is happening here that she should have seen before. But Terri is not nearly as frightened as Alyssa—Alyssa who is clinging to her barrel cactus as if it were a life raft—oh, woeful life raft, so small and unlikely to save anyone from the mercury flow of recollection, the dinners, the stealth orgasms, the sweet conversations, the money, her relationship with Zero in its entirety.

"Well, lookee here," says Zero. "It's Alyssa, from the office. Hi, Alyssa. Nice cactus you've got yourself there."

Could all the ladies be friends? Why couldn't Hanna, Alyssa, Sarah, and Terri, so cheerful and good-natured, each one gorgeous in her own way, and certainly aware of the vicissitudes of being female, of the specifically *female* experience, whether that has to do with one's period, or one's first crush, or one's first poem in a literary magazine, be pals, be—in the sisterhood of the traveling pants or whatever the hell? Sarah and Terri, in fact, ran the Susan G. Komen Race for the Cure earlier this year, the very same race Hanna was in, although she was walking. Hanna had just heard the news about her own body, and the injustice was still sinking in, the idea that someone out *there* could tell you about something in *here*. She was, after an initial day of torpor, rather adrenaline-driven, and so the walk was good for her (as were the pink ribbon pins and a host of new Listserv subscriptions and chat rooms). At first, the race was overwhelming: droves of women and some men and a few kids with their faces painted or holding up signs—*I'm walking for my Grandma* and *Find a Cure!*—streaming across Reid Park, gathering under an arch of a thousand pink, brown, and white balloons; a frightening DJ standing on top of a ladder; shrill, distorted voices coming out of speakers the size of vans; people clambering over the hill, their inevitable multifarious movements evoking a hoard of insects running across a kitchen floor. It was scary. One woman fell, and Hanna helped her get up. That's when Hanna almost cried, catching this woman's eye. The woman had the fuzzies—her hair was growing back, but like a chick's downy feathers. Then the woman stumbled forward and disappeared into the crowd. Hanna and her posse (Hanna has a posse! But so many did, or so it seemed. There was "Breast Cancer Boot Camp," a dozen women in fatigues. On the corner of Broadway, the sergeant blew a whistle and her troops did some sketchy push-ups on a bank's lawn. There was a Native American contingent, and a whole bunch of people wearing T-shirts for "Mama Jones.") found their place in the crowd, holding hands, which felt almost necessary for safety, and she felt a surge of goodwill and companionship, and they marched in the rising heat along the chain link fence festooned with bras of all shapes, sizes, and colors, hooked together and stretched for virtually a mile.

But that was then, and Hanna is certainly feeling a lack of companionability now, feeling no sisterhood here at Tohono Chul Park, the saguaro diseased and deformed, a single arm extending on one side, the "head" itself skewed, not something she even thought possible in saguaros, as if the unnatural was natural or condoned at this point, the way things were going overall.

The entire world withers when Alyssa timidly answers Zero, "Hi, Mr. Daitch."

It isn't as if Hanna hasn't endured other affairs. But that was before the cancer, and also, as far as this particular woman is concerned, they've already gone over this. They went over it when Hanna discovered the texts, including the photo of Alyssa's young smiling face embedded in the extraterrestrial square of his phone's screen, a little, beautiful face from another world. And it isn't that Hanna necessarily hates women at this moment, or this woman in particular. But it is like that, too. She hates women and this woman and breasts and men and even the *concept* of a saguaro that doesn't do what it's supposed to, the lift into the sky, a sentinel's noble shape, pure upward motion. She hates how everything gets ruined, how ruin runs through her veins like chemo, how there are forces and then there are *forces*, how before you know it, something is being killed and something is living and it's just a crapshoot after all. No God. No, no, not here, not in the desert, not at Tohono Chul, not now.

Zero is smiling affably but resolutely, as if his lips are pinned back by dental tools.

The black-haired one is not smiling the way she did on the cell phone, her head turned to one side, smiling into the camera as if she were a co-ed, another kind of life force, really quite gorgeous, and they aren't all gorgeous, and it doesn't matter if they are gorgeous, to Hanna. Or not that much, in the final analysis.

"I thought this was such a nice cactus," Alyssa says. *I thought there really was a Santa Claus.*

"Damn nice cactus," Zero says. "Must be heavy though. Surely." And he makes a slight motion, as if to help her, but then stops short.

"So you're Alyssa," says Hanna. "It's not what I expected, to meet you like this. I thought you would just disappear, like a little puff of smoke."

Alyssa's fingers are tight and jointed in an arachnid tangle around the pot. Her vibrant French manicure, the robust shine, the symmetry of ten.

"But you didn't."

No, thinks Alyssa, I didn't. Remembering Mrs. Daitch at the Chartreuse Spa, how invisible Alyssa was, how close they were.

"You fucked my husband while I was getting chemo and radiation treatments. You. Fucked. My. Husband. While—"

"Now, Hanna," says Zero, taking hold of his wife's Toulouse-Lautrec arm. "Let's not make a scene, for Christ's sake."

Impossible to tell whether Zero is looking at Hanna or at Alyssa. It's the glasses, hard to see through them, and his head angle is slightly demented—more demented than his loafers, which live in a world of sanity. The sanity of the dollar bill, the sanity of the underworld, the sanity of definition, the sanity of absence, the sanity of history, the sanity of nothing, like the way the Tucson sky can feel—a place of nothing, not even the tiniest drop of rain.

Sarah is upset. She's upset because marriages are being fucked with. She's upset because she brought Alyssa and Terri here and she's upset because she has to go back to work tomorrow and she's upset because nothing is resolved. She was going to buy a *Bulbine* or an aloe for next to the hose by her front door, and there was going to be something good in that, in cutting the ground with her shovel, breaking through, grinding the earth into rubble and pointing the nozzle in that direction and letting the water flow. But that will not happen now, or if it does, she won't enjoy it, or if she does enjoy it, it will only be part of a larger whole, a whole that includes this. What is in front of her, in front of them all: Alyssa's face turning pink in the sun.

Hanna looks at Zero, and her mouth closes in a resolute line of disappointment. She had her own stealth orgasms with him, back in the day. They've raised two children. They respect each other. They have grown together; they're growing old together now. Everything is both eternal and just on the razor's edge of disappearing, she wants to say. Don't fuck with it. But she knows that she will never get through to him, that Zero feels most of all that he can outwit mortality itself, and who is she to deny him that single, overriding pleasure? For despite his wealth and position in the world, she knows who he is. She knows the body of Zero. She knows the nighttime Zero, the day in, day out Zero, the Zero who cherished his mother, the Zero who does not sleep, the Zero who rails against stupidity, the Zero who has leapt over impediments. Finally, he is Zero, her husband, and she hesitates to take away from him that which he imagines is there.

It was lonesome at the resort up in Phoenix. Every day, the quiet women in their tan clothes rubbing her with their small hands. Hanna's face nestled in the massage table's hole. Her tears fell two and a half feet and landed on the carpet underneath, resting on the synthetic fibers, unabsorbed. The candles, the trickling sound of the tabletop water fountain, the Native American–style soundtrack coming through the speakers. All a kind of consolation, and yet no consolation at all. The women who gave her the oxygen boost and the vitamin-infusion facial and the detoxifying treatment were not people to her then, but tools. And now Hanna doesn't even feel Zero's hand on her arm. She doesn't see or feel anything, and in that, she, too, is immortal. She unbelongs to the savage sun and the xeriscape garden and the controversy on the path involving, somehow, Zero and all three of these women.

Terri takes Alyssa's arm in her own. The younger woman's body is thrumming with anxiety. Wrongness is a kind of power, an essential element, but nonetheless here, under the flattening sun, Alyssa has lost an animating dream she once had, a vision that had included real life, but also included an ineffable something she and Zero had created between them, out of nothing. Now that nothing has crashed back. Her life will be ordinary again. It wasn't ordinary yet, because of the anger and the drama, but it will be ordinary soon. Maybe by this evening, certainly by tomorrow morning.

"C'mon," says Terri. She leads Alyssa, in the gentlest way, to a wider patch in the path, past the saguaro that leans, as if it no longer believes in the sun, to the wedge of gravel between this path and the tent where the succulents are lined up, exotics all, shih tzus and Pomeranians and dachshunds, their heads up, alert, hopeful, and, for the moment, protected against the elements and against the mauling of amateur gardeners, those with quick fixes in mind, with brief and passionate inspiration.

The Golden Promise of Flight and Good Wishes

Howie's wings are stitched to his golden cap, and if he turns his head quickly, they swing in his eyes, reminding him of their power. He's wearing a knee-length dinosaur-green cape made of metallic fabric, and because he's on the corpulent side, or because the cape is maybe even a child's size, anyone can see his jeans and his Wildcats Final Four T-shirt (bought at Savers by his mother). Wings flapping like a golden retriever's ears, he still embodies his character.

But what is he? Is he a dinosaur, an angel, a god, a wrestling champ? This isn't clear—not to Howie, not to the people driving past him on the corner of Speedway and Country Club, not even to the stressed shady guy who hired him a week ago. "Like it matters? You're a messenger. The message is happiness, see? They look at you and they're thinking: fun, friendly, party time. Don't talk on your phone while you're out there. Fun people don't talk to other people on the phone. Don't pick your nose or scratch your balls. No one's paying you to scratch your balls, bongo. So do you have it in you? Do you have it in you, Mr. Howie?"

Howie had been unemployed for five months. Fuck yes, he had it in him.

"Hey!" Howie shouts, targeting the first car stopped at the light, heading north on Country Club. "Final days! Last call for alcohol! Wait, party girl, let's get it going, we've got something going on here! Hey, family man, I've got the plan! Free stuff, free connection, free goods, free gifts, we've got the free stuff, man, we've got it. Hey cutie! Hey, come on by, last weeks, final days! Fifty percent off, you know it's a deal. It's a steal, people. Fifty percent! Fifty percent! Final days! Final days!"

When the light turns green and all the drivers muttering and ignoring him, sitting behind tinted glass, scowling, pissed off, talking into headsets or texting into their laps, begin to shuttle forward and away, out of his life forever, Howie turns his attention back to Speedway and executes a more generalized wave and shout.

Mostly people just zigzag around Tucson all day, unemployed and at loose ends, like he is, or was. There's the east-west relay race between Costco at Grant and Wilmot and the Auto Mall on Wetmore and Oracle, and then your competing brain-fried scream through town on I-10. Some losers don't go the distance, ants who didn't get the message from the queen ant or whatever, trundling on out to 7-Eleven and back, or to the Goodwill or Sonic. An aerial shot of their lives would be a bunch of squiggles, like when you back yourself into a corner on an Etch A Sketch, or if you're tracking the progress of that old confused ant, half dead on a spurt of Raid, trying to find his way back to his little crumb before someone's boot stomps his ass.

The sign is heavy now, two hours into his shift. He still spins it and performs the *shazam!* move widely known in the dinosaur kingdom, but overall, Howie probably isn't as spry as he was at noon.

"Yo, twinkle toes! Where you gonna fly to? Take me with you!" shouts a woman. She's not in a car—she's hanging over the wall of the patio at Chuy's, twenty feet back from where he's standing. Howie hung out at Chuy's once or twice, years ago. Most recently he just snuck in to use the facilities. A faux roadhouse kind of deal, it's Baja in the desert: plastic sharks hanging from the ceiling, funny (not) graffiti, pitcher specials, a bunch of lard-ass Harley-Davidson types, and all manner of fakery and bullshit, more Ron Paul than Obama.

The woman's got one arm stretched out in front of her, cigarette in hand. A thin blond ponytail trails over her shoulder. Her body is lazy. He can hear the rasp in her voice from where he's standing, and the silence after the question. Two guys sit back in black T-shirts, leading with their bellies. It's the women you have to look out for.

He's sweating like a bear. He wipes his forehead, but it slicks back up as soon as his hand falls. The sidewalk twinkles with glass. Shards, fragments, beads—glass shattered into a million pieces, and bits of metal, too. There had to have been an accident here, or a few over the years. A handmade cross is stuck in the ground by the signal pole, one arm broken off. It could also be the skeleton of a previous sign holder's sign—some guy who dropped the sign and fled the fuck out of here! But it's good to have a job. It's not just good—it's amazing. He's ignoring the bitch from Chuy's and her friends, even though he can hear them chuckling behind him now. In his pocket is his forbidden phone with the message (or two or three messages) from his mother. A buzz tickles his thigh, abrupt even here on the noisy intersection. Of all people, his mother is probably happiest about this job, because as much as she loves him (he sounds out the words in his head: *as much as she loves him, she loves him*), she'll be happy when he gets on his feet again. She maybe doesn't finally *want* him sleeping on the couch in the living room, though he's pretty considerate about everything: folding his sheets and blanket, getting groceries, even paying her electric bill that one time. She push-pulls, and that's what pisses him off. He's surely the fuck on his feet now. Literally.

"Hey there, sweetie! Check it out! We've got ourselves some serious bargaining power. Serious, my lady friend! Come on by! You know we love you. *Woo-hoo*, you are a beautiful person. A beautiful person! Bye now! Bye-bye, blackbird! Bye-bye, bye-bye."

He ends in a weird Southern accent, he doesn't know where that came from, and he laughs for a second—to himself, of course (none other than). Shit, he *liked* the smell of car exhaust when he was a kid. He liked the smell of gas. This job's perfect for him! Speedway Boulevard = Memory Lane. Yup, born in this town. Tucson's finest, he thinks for a brief proud-bitter moment, remembering all the ways his luck has dogged him.

"Hey honey, can I ask you something?" shouts the blond. He ignores her again.

Red light, green light, go. He turns away from the SUV, two trucks, and a sedan, and heads back to the Country Club side of the intersection. You don't want to just shout right at the window because people freak. Catch their eye from a moderate distance.

"We've got it going on, we've got all that you need, everything is here, right in front of you, here I am."

"You got a permit or something, like? Because a handsome dude like you, in the twinkle-toes outfit, right? Public menace. Menace to society!"

The patio crowd bursts into laughter. An awful cackle from the bitch chicks, and a huffing pre-emphysema hack from the men.

From the side of the street, you can see the mountains. The Catalinas are always there, in the background, but they keep receding from view the longer you look at them, a zero-sum game.

Marissa stares out from the passenger seat of her friend's car at the man. He is frightening. He reminds her of some guys, some parties. Probably it's the way he leans over from the sidewalk and shouts, letting his gaze follow as the car rumbles forward. It's the way he leans and finds your eyes and looks right into them. What is he advertising, anyway? Some kind of liquidation sale, or is it a job? She grinds her head into the back of the seat, waiting for the light to change. He searches you out. Aggressive is what he is. Marissa pulls her hands out from where they were squeezed between her legs and folds them against her chest and looks down. The violence of the world is creeping in, stomping closer to where she is. Stores are closing, deals to be had, rock bottom discount, call to action.

From the driver's seat, Marissa's friend: "So I'm like telling him I got it the first time, I know he has these issues, right? They've been there from the beginning, I mean he let it be known pretty clearly, it's like this founding principle of our relationship. The fact is he's vulnerable, *so vulnerable*, he's got this whole set of issues that always need to be taken care of, he's a broken puppy. And I really haven't minded, for whatever reason, because I love him, see what I mean? He's straight-up honest about everything else, I guess that's part of it. But finally, *finally*—and it's weird this came to me in the middle of a movie, it's not like I think my *life* should be a movie, made in Hollywood or a fairy tale or whatever, but a person needs more than this, for fuck's sake. Right? Hello? Earth to Marissa? It's like, can you really have a relationship where there's one thing that's actually *immovable*, like a boulder in the middle of the living room? I mean, you move to Europe, right, and you have to pack the boulder. You go on a canoe ride, there's that damn boulder. Christmas? A big tree, some presents, a big old boulder. Something's got to give. That's just the way life is. You can't change that about life, see what I mean?"

"Do you see that guy out there? He looks like a creep," says Marissa.

"Where? Oh, that guy. What's he selling—cameras?"

"Cameras? I think it's a store closing or something." Marissa's eyes are trained on the dashboard now; she's avoiding the look of the dinosaur-hero-messenger man. She's in a box. She's in solitary. She's in a barrel and she's no Houdini and she's about to explode, about to go postal ballistic, she's a cat in a bag, a dead canary.

"Crazy," says Marissa's friend, then she turns back to the road. Marissa looks back up. A meth blond in some yesteryear style of jeans and a black tank top has jumped the patio wall and is making her way over to the guy with the sign. She's creeping over the gravel, weaving around mounds of yellow lantana and agave, coming closer like a cartoon spy. She keeps looking back at the people hanging over the Chuy's patio wall. She's hunched and creeping; you can practically see her knobbed spine like a thin monkey's, her face distorted into a mask of hilarity, hostility. The dinosaur superhero wheels around. Monkey lady puts her hands in her pockets and squints at him, big smile like they're long-ago buddies running into each other at an airport or on a pier. She's so thin. The jeans are '80s vintage, thick denim Levi's, up to her belly button. Arms tensile and brown from the Arizona sun.

Marissa's friend presses the gas pedal and the Accord whines at a higher pitch, but they miss the light a second time. She starts talking again, her words a smothering balloon. The sign man's chest is puffed out of the dinosaur outfit; his belly is showing. His face is red and shiny and crumpled, the sign at an unreadable angle. He's just a fat fuck, the blond is thinking. She's asking her audience to agree, those on the patio and those on the street. Whatever she's saying, the man's not happy about it. He's staring at her. Now she's got her cigarette in her mouth and she's pulling a wad of bills out of her pocket. She looks back at the woman and two men at the bar and winks in a dramatic pantomime. She pulls off a dollar and gets it all smooth and holds it up. Dinosaur man looks at it, too. She flings the dollar onto the gravel between them. He looks sad, like someone ripped the ear off his stuffed bunny, and then he jumps. He picks it up. She gestures to her gang and they're laughing and she is, too. Now she edges up to the side of the street, peels off a second bill. It's a twenty, maybe. It could be a twenty. Cigarette standing up in her mouth, she holds the bill by both ends like a magician showing off, and then she rushes toward sorry-ass dinosaur dog man, flaps the bill at him, and flings it into the street. With great strides, she hustles back toward Chuy's. Dinosaur man—he doesn't think. He doesn't hesitate. He runs out onto Speedway and swipes at the bill. He misses it. The wind moves the bill another three feet away and he lurches forward, his sneakers too big, cape falling to one side. His winged cap stays on—he must use bobby pins to hold those pretty little wings. Now the blond looks back, incredulous. Dinosaur man is stumbling over his feet. He falls on the road as a tan SUV runs the yellow light and attempts to haul ass through the intersection, heading east. Marissa screams.

In another, better world, Howie puts the twenty in his pocket and adjusts his cape. The side of his face burns. His hands, too. He picks up his sign and walks back to the side of the road and stands for a minute, gathering strength. Howie's heart is going fast, all messed up, not regular at all—that was a close call, all right! The tan SUV is long gone, by now as far as Swan, idling in front of Magpies. The Chuy's crowd has disappeared, maybe gone inside. He takes a deep breath, steadies himself. He waves at a purple SUV and a white truck. Two silver Hondas in a row, a white Kia. With the twenty, he'll buy his mom something, those chocolate turtles she likes. He likes them, too. They go pretty well with beer—it's the nuts, he thinks. He'll buy them for her and he'll go over on a Sunday night and they'll watch *The Amazing Race* or something—one Sunday after he's moved out, when he's just visiting. A BMW full of sorority girls rumbles up, all four sitting straight up like Barbies. They don't look at him; it's like he doesn't exist. Next: a mother and father with a kid in the back. Some kind of dorky retard kid, something wrong with him, anyway. The kid looks at Howie and Howie shakes his sign at him. "The end is near!" he will shout. "The end is near, you little scum bucket!"

Tasks

1. As a baby, to kill the two serpents swarming your crib.

A word must be said about Harry's parents, who were, first of all, amateur campers, but in all other ways considered themselves a hip and cosmopolitan couple. They fought frequently—outlandish, public-forum dramas—but always somehow resolved things in the end, so the marriage seemed to last (in their minds, and in the minds of those who knew them) forever.

The campsite on Mount Lemmon had a barbeque grill, but they had forgotten lighter fluid, and so they did not eat the hot dogs, but dined exclusively on rolls with ketchup, potato chips, and two warm beers (for them, a kitschy Roughing It moment). Probably due to the lack of audience, they tired early of their ranting and raving and by nine-thirty had hit the sack, an air mattress in the tent. Little Harry—so hefty for a ten-month-old, like a baby javelina—slept beside them in his portable crib. It was his mother who woke in the bleak gray morning to discover the boy sitting on one side of the crib, sucking his thumb, the eviscerated snakes/ now snake skins besmirched with brown ooze lying inert on the other side of the plastic-topped mattress.

2. To act out against the music teacher, as if turning your back on all good things and simultaneously tempting fate.

The music teacher was, for all intents and purposes, a pain in the ass, but nonetheless, there was no need to kill the poor man. And it was unfortunate, surely, to have this much strength and not know how to control it. Harry hadn't performed well on the scales, and there was something in the little snorty noise the music teacher made that always made him feel as if the room were much, much too small (the room *was* small, and soundproof, too—no one heard the screams), and this is what he was feeling in the nanosecond before *it* occurred. Something snapped. Regular safe normal reality took five, and the snorty music teacher was a shaking mess, he was toast, utterly and completely toast. It was all briefly exhilarating, but Harry felt culpability and horror and regret as he let the limp body fall back against the wall, next to the forgotten saxophone and the toppled music stand.

3. To be made insane.

Would it be trite to blame his mother? But she was always getting in his business. The music teacher's death had nearly destroyed Harry; it made him perpetually tremble. For many years, he would have no will to live. He would be bad company to himself. "I am a bad seed, a bad boy," Harry whispered in the bathroom, "and someday I will be a bad man, too." Somehow he'd emerge from this morass of self-hate and begin to rebuild what was left of his life. Still, by all accounts, his childhood was a difficult one. He was always pummeling his young friends. He had no real interests, no girlfriends. He equated his mother's presence with an echo, echoing. A radiation, radiating.

4. To kill your own children.

But back to the music teacher and his untoward passing. For a whole month afterward, Harry stayed in his bedroom. The first few days, the noise from within came in waves, scorched-earth breakage and crunching and ripping, accompanied by Harry's own howls and shouts. Terrible for the compassionate ear—but his parents did not listen. They were powerful people: they believed in their own acts. And even if his father wasn't one hundred percent down with his wife's level of panic-stricken control-freakhood, he shrugged his shoulders (eternal guilt and wrongdoing dogged him like that, allowed her free rein) and turned his back on his son. After those first few days, the noise level went down. It was silent, ominously so. By that time, Harry had already burned his saxophone compositions, those he'd painstakingly and in atonement written as an homage to Jerry, the music teacher, those compositions that actually were tremendously powerful, emotional and eloquent and melodic and haunting. And yet he burned them all and resolved to take a different path. Harry's life as a musician and composer was put to a tragic, early halt.

5. *To serve ten years as a slave, tasking for a weak man on the advice of your mother, ten years, which does indeed translate as a long time for anyone.*

Here we must acknowledge Harry's mom's decade-long devotion to one Dr. Eurosmith, a weak yet powerful man, the leader of his own pathetic cult. Cults. There's always something deeply dreary about them, is it not so? From the outside, it seems clear: what *were* those people thinking? And yet Hanna wasn't the type to enter the sweat lodge *herself*, or to take the unfortunate oily substance for depression *herself*, or to relegate *herself* to the bathroom with a week's worth of enema formulas. She was more of an insider, a silent partner, a steady and important promoter of Dr. Eurosmith and his ways. Privately some have speculated that Hanna Daitch and Loren Eurosmith may have had an affair of some kind, a mutually beneficial event or series of events. In any case, we have to grimly acknowledge that Hanna may *not* have been completely cultified, but that this was all her actual and conscious choice. That she simply used Dr. Eurosmith. She used people. It was her prerogative. She found the way she could help them (money usually worked, influence wasn't bad either), and then she entered the arrangement, as a queen might embark an ocean liner.

6. *To slay the lion.*

Or to put it another way, to become a man. These were the words Dr. Eurosmith used with poor young Harry—still pimple-chinned, beard so wispy it was ridiculous—in the confines of the doctor's excellently appointed office, mahogany and red leather furniture, Frank Lloyd Wright–inspired overall, some Navajo rugs and other Native American artifacts tucked into nooks or flattened behind glass. Best feature: one complete wall a window, a twenty-by-twenty-five-foot pane of glass overlooking Saguaro National Park. Did Harry *want* to become a man? Because despite his muscles—and here the middle-aged doctor allowed himself a glance at the boy's pectorals, at the heaving round sweep of his shoulders, even as Harry shredded a Kleenex and snorted snot and as tears rolled down his oily visage—Harry was not a man. *He was not a man.* He wouldn't be, either, unless he proved it. Proved it one way or another. Proved it ten times. His mother wanted him to prove himself, was that not so? And if he did prove himself, maybe his father would notice also. But it didn't matter about either of them, Dr. Eurosmith said, suddenly passionate and whispery, holding Harry's knees in his own tanned, be-ringed hands. "It matters what you think, Harry. What you think, and what I think, too. Young Harry. Young, young Harry. Are you afraid of me?" Dr. Eurosmith unbuttoned his shirt, fluffing it to the back a bit, to expose his waxed chest. And then there was the unbuttoning of his pants and the unzipping. (It was for reasons other than sexual desire that Dr. Eurosmith performed this ritual, he would later claim.) "Are you afraid?" he repeated, his oddly long erection a black sickle against the bright glass wall—behind which all of the desert lived. "No," whispered Harry.

7. *To kill a nine-headed hydra, not to mention a bad giant crab sent to help the hydra—the hydra, not you!—by your mother.*

Well, you know how it is with hydras. Their heads are always regrowing. But it's not like this was a real hydra, per se, not in the twenty-first century! We have shielded ourselves from such things with distance, the great leveler called history. But ask Harry—ask Harry if hydras exist. Ask if it isn't so that when he finally lopped the ninth head off, by contract the final and last hydra head around, and as it was looking, *really* looking like he might defeat the monster—*she* sent in the crab. Ask him and he'll tell you, though it may take a little jogging of his memory, as Harry has put some of the degradations and difficulties related to his mother in a very very small memory closet right on the very very edge of the cliff of nothingness, the cliff of escape, and so it's hard to recall, and some of the nine-headed type memories have already been ejected completely, are lost in space.

8. *To kill a wild boar.*

By college graduation, Harry was fast becoming an alcoholic. One night he was sitting at a bar downtown, a place he often went to drown his sorrows and watch basketball and have a few appetizers, when who but the lanky research assistant, a friend of a friend, took a seat next to him, and proceeded to talk about his travails in the dating world. All his travails. All his fits and starts—in fact, all the absolute nothing that was his love life, this sad sack fellow, this absolutely boring man. And yet nonetheless he found a way to fill the air space around Harry with his tales of non-love

and even non-sex. At about midnight, Harry exploded. Don't hold it
against him, but yes, he exploded—and he shut that man up in the most
terrible and absolute fashion. Quite the messy scene. No sense this would
really help with Harry's own lack-of-love life in the end. For less than a
second, though, strength seemed to mean something.

*9. As a break from all that, land creatures and their kind, to be attacked by but
then to drive away a swarm of dangerous birds.*

That's what the headaches were like, and it wasn't as if he got rid of them
forever. In fact, he didn't get rid of them at all. He simply persevered.
The headaches were sharp and metallic, and they came from the sky and
from lights and from breezes; they came as dark birds out of the bright
nowhere. He held his hands over his face, he shielded his body with his
arms, he fell to one knee, and the birds attacked, and in the attack was a
lifetime of song, and then the attack was over, the skies were still, and he
was alive. He could go on.

10. To capture a sacred deer.

Women had always been a problem, and it wasn't completely because of
Harry's...dubious...challenging...relationship to his mother. (And let's
not forget Poppykins, frolicking about with other women day and night,
in costume no less, probably driving his wife mad at the same time as his
son.) But then, while waiting at a snack stand at one of Dr. Eurosmith's
seminars, Harry met a young woman—one of the tech crew setting up
the stage and sound system. She was a thin person in skinny jeans and
a long striped T-shirt, her black hair up in a scrambled bun with a fake
bone stuck in the middle. He thought the bone was funny. He liked it.
She turned to look at him, and that was when he felt all of a sudden more
courageous than before. Courageous in the face of something daunting.
Courageous in the face of gentleness. He wanted to take her in his arms,
to whisper something to her—something he really meant, something not
about him, for fuck's sake. He wanted to tell her how lovely she was, or
something about the world at large, like the purple flowers he discovered
on the moors on his way to slay the hydra, or the lifestyles of dangerous
birds, how they care for their young for the whole first year of life. What
he did is he said hello. At first she simply regarded him, her eyes lidded,
sleepy looking, and then her mouth trembled into a small, welcoming

smile, and she said hello back. Maybe it was because he kept staring, but she asked him what was up.

"I'm just getting a cookie or something. Between classes," he said, faltering.

"You're, like, a participant?"

He said he was.

"Man," she said, worrying off the cap to her bottle of water. "I'm concerned about some of you people. Folks will do just about anything for this guy."

"I know what you mean," said Harry, anxiously taking his cookie and pocketing the change.

"What is it about him, anyway? He just seems like a run-of-the-mill charlatan. I mean, I don't want to dis him, since you must be kind of into it and all."

Here we are, thought Harry, just two people hanging out in the sunshine. She didn't know he was a hero in the making—that his heroism was killing him.

"He offers people a way to look at themselves. He offers them . . . a way to look at life, like you can use it and not let it use you . . ." Harry trailed off, aware he was appropriating their language. Dr. Eurosmith's language.

She shook her head, and the bone bobbed in the raven nest. "I don't get it."

"I don't completely get it either. Actually, I'm baffled by it."

Harry smiled. He felt wretched. He didn't know what had come over him.

"Well, I'm Cindy."

"Hi, Cindy. I'm Harry."

The sun was making griddle cakes of both of them.

After a pause, he said, "So—what are you doing here, then?"

"I work with the sound team. Those dudes." She gestured to a few prehistoric types hovering with bad posture over by a van.

"That sounds cool."

Now the moment had come: Cindy was about to walk out on him. Harry knew that you needed to be gentle. He knew this in some hidden vestibule of his soul, a place he'd made all on his own, not with any help from Dr. Eurosmith or his mother or father, or any of the relentless crowds who seemed to, already, expect something of him.

"I like that—that hair thing," he said.

"Thanks."

"I've never met a woman with a bone in her hair before."

"First time for everything, right?"

"Yeah."

"All right, have a good seminar," she said, raising her water bottle in salute and taking one skinny-jeaned Converse-sneakered step away from him.

"Wait—" said Harry, and she did. She turned.

And so it began. A whole new raft of challenges awaited Harry, now that he had found something of patience, or necessary action, within.

11. To clean up an inordinate amount of shit.

It happened metaphorically and actually. He got a job, his first job, at Rillito Park. Harry had a low-key but persistent interest in horses. When he told his father, Zero just shrugged and turned back to what he was doing, reading the stock report on his iPhone and picking his nose, on the other side of the magnificent marble kitchen island. His mother— he didn't talk to her about it beforehand. He knew better. Well, he did, at least for a few minutes, know better. It was always like that for Harry. He'd make some kind of progress as a human being and then backtrack. It was the backtracking that plagued him, that seemed genuine, as opposed to the anomalous progress moments, those exultations. His father just shrugged when Harry told him about the job as "assistant stable manager" (i.e., shit shoveler). The full-on shit shovelers were inevitably Mexican, sometimes nominally Mexican American, but the zoned-out racetrack manager had looked at Harry with what seemed like apathy but was actually approbation, shrugged, and given him the job. He didn't care who Harry's father was: this was a first. And so on a cold (for Tucson) and sunny morning, Harry parked his (nicer than the other employees') car in the dusty lot and walked around the old-fashioned stadium to the stable. He was alive with anticipation, as he had been with Cindy from the sound company, a brief feeling of almost-happiness. The horses arrived in unwieldy, rumbling trailers. To Harry, they were nothing like any of the beasts he'd encountered so far. They were an alternate reality, reminding him of a life that wasn't his to live—or maybe it was, maybe it could be! This he felt deeply as the big animals walked by, as he kicked at the shavings in the staging ring's stalls and pulled string from a bushel of hay, letting the scratchy cloud sigh open.

By noon the stands were full, gambling had begun, and the horses were stressing out. The smell of hot dogs and tacos and fried dough mingled with the shit smell and the frantic wind of people and the monotonous cheer of the barker, who could have been Howdy Doody he was so non-real. First race was a Quarter Horse half mile. Twelve horses in the ring, and Harry assistant-managing his sweet ass off. It was exhilarating—a real job! Harry had long ago lost his adolescent fat (he'd been a pudgy kid), and that winter at the racetrack, he became taller and thinner and stronger than ever before. He was sorry when the season ended. He'd liked the job, even though he knew it wasn't his destiny. When he watched the horses loading up after the last race in April, he felt a little like he'd always be lonely.

12. To fetch a favorite golden girdle from the queen of the Amazons, and yet in so doing, to kill her. Theoretically to have gotten the golden girdle anyway.

He was cosmically shocked when Cindy said yes, she'd come to Easter dinner. At twenty-one, he'd never invited a girl to his house before. Not that he and Cindy were officially dating. So far, their relationship had been a friendship, unfolding at coffee shops and comic book stores. She'd turned him on to Miyazaki, the Japanese filmmaker.

There they were, his parents, surrounded by platters that had come in by FedEx only yesterday: Scottish toffee made from lamb's blood and whiskey, coconut cake made fluffy and delicious by the last known slaves in the world, pecans dusted with gold dust, Belgian cocoa in dissolvable spun-sugar sachets.

Harry had worried all week. *I didn't do this for her, but for me.* He thought that his family might damage her mental health with some kind of nuclear jujitsu, as only his family could pull off. Cindy was a no-bullshit type person, as she'd hastened to point out. And he believed her. Cindy, with the bone in her hair, or some other bauble, and then one day she went ahead and got a Mohawk (alarming for Harry, but he went with it). Cindy, with the dark eyeliner and soft voice and love for Japanese film-makers. Now he was going to subject her to old Zeus and Hera (as he jokingly referred to them). It might well be too much too soon—he was obviously rushing things. And yet did he want to *keep* them from her, a kind of lie itself? Most of all he was worried she'd run screaming out of his life. Despite the Mohawk and the no-bullshit and the very cool demeanor, he knew she was a delicate person, after all.

The patio was laden with goods, his parents at the center.

"Guys, this is Cindy. Cindy—my mom and dad," he said cheerfully, in a ventriloquist's parody of his younger self.

"So glad you could join us," said his mother.

"Hello, Cindy," his father said in a familiar, appraising tone.

Laurabell was in her room.

Cindy said hello and then stood there, holding her arm at the elbow. He got them both Cokes from the outside refrigerator, and they sat together on the indoor-outdoor furniture, enjoying the dissipating and scurrilous wafts of mist from the mechanism overhead. Maria, the cleaning woman and cook, came out to speak to his mother. Zero was taking what appeared to be a last glance at his phone.

Harry smiled at Cindy. He felt sweatier of palm and drier of mouth than he had been since their first coffee at Raging Sage, five months before. All the intervening comic book store forays and that one time he brought her to the racetrack disappeared. It was as if the moment when he almost touched her hand and the almost-touch was better than a real touch even was also gone.

"So you're in film, huh? That's what this character said," his father said congenially, having placed his phone on the table. He leaned forward. His head was at a high polish, and he was wearing a black linen shirt Harry hadn't seen before.

"Very peripheral. I do sound and lighting, tech stuff."

"So how did you meet this kid? He doesn't get out much. He's a shy boy." Zero smiled briefly and reached for the gilt nuts.

"We met at Dr. Eurosmith's, like, seminar? I was working, and he was I guess just there."

Cindy! He could tell *she* was feeling shy, and he was preternaturally aware of the bullying approach of his father. Hanna had dispensed with Maria's questions and resumed watching the conversation.

"Oh, fuck, Eurosmith? My wife's in love with that man. Thinks he understands something about human nature that she can't get right here, right around the couch with us. She loves it all. The trance sessions, the hogums and the pilgrims and—"

"It's a *hogan,* Zero," Hanna said.

"Hogum, hogan. Who gives a fuck? If I wanted to sweat, I'd walk into a steam room at the gym. But it does you good, doesn't it, sweetheart? It does you good, working with that charlatan."

"He's not a charlatan," Hanna said stiffly, then smiled at Cindy. This was less than a year before Hanna would be diagnosed with breast cancer. Cindy smiled back in a non-smile kind of way, and after she smiled thusly, she did not for quite a long time look back at Harry. Harry finished his

Coke and opened another. His father got a call and stood for twenty minutes over by the pool. Cindy was nodding at something his mother was saying. Harry was having trouble hearing: his ears had stopped up and he couldn't tell if they were talking about shopping or the new wine bar at La Encantada or about sorority life then and now.

By the time Maria and her helper (a sister? a cousin?) served dinner in the solarium—a long, unique room with French doors leading out to a secondary patio overlooking the Catalinas, the mountains from this close range looking simply like a swath of texture—others had arrived. People from work, and so-called friends (Harry couldn't remember their names or how he knew them). Seven-year-old Laurabell, his favorite person in the room, sat near their mother.

"Having fun so far?" Harry said under his breath to Cindy.

She raised her eyebrows, and he felt the delicate horror of implication. He reached for the wine and waited for the toast—to a surpassingly excellent winter, and to riches to come. Dinner itself went quickly. Besides the FedExed items, there were the goslings that Maria had feathered and deboned and fricasseed in truffle oil. The tiny bird bodies were perched, like lynching victims, atop wild mushroom and spinach risotto. As if they were in little nests, Hanna pointed out.

In the unregulated lull between dinner and dessert, Harry found his father and Cindy in the hall. He knew with 100% certainty that Cindy was not *doing* anything, but was being *done to*, in that Zero way that Harry had witnessed since he was young and had come to loathe. It was a good, fiery loathing, although also not that good after all. There Zero was, cornering another woman in another hall. Up against the bona fide Matisse print went Cindy's Mohawked head and her gingham shirt, '50s lovely. From this distance, from this horrible angle, Harry could see a fist of extra fabric—the black linen shirt come up like a little puppet through the unzipped pants—and the ever-seeking, ever-hungry member of his father.

"No!" cried Harry.

Zero's head swung around. "For Christ's sake, give me a break. Get out of here. Get lost, son."

"Get away from her," said Harry, his voice thick as he stumbled toward the two, tripping over a fold in the Oriental runner.

His father turned, zipping up. "You're a stupid ass," he said to his son. "Can't anyone have privacy in this house?"

Zero walked away—and there was Cindy. She was trembling. The not-happiness of what happened had ruined everything.

"Are you okay? What an asshole," said Harry.

When he tried to brush a tear from her cheek, she whipped her head in the other direction. He took a step back. She said, "Take me home, Harry."

13. To capture four man-eating mares.

A man-eating mare. That's hilarious. Who'd ever call girls in bars man-eating mares? He didn't call them that. He didn't call them anything. And what happened didn't even feel like sex; it felt like nothing, although obviously his body had made *something* happen. He felt like some old asshole on Viagra. His penis worked, but that was about it. How depressing it all was. The body a machine, his heart ruined, Cindy not calling him back. His last view of her, face streaked with black eyeliner. The way she slammed the shit out of his car door when he dropped her off at her apartment complex behind Whole Foods.

14. Jesus fucking Christ, would his labors ever end? Because after he caught the fire-breathing bull on Crete and also wrangled up a huge herd of red cows belonging to a major monster with three bodies and spindly little legs and a bad-ass dog, he still had two more tasks, because fucking mother-goddess decreed it was so. Because his love, actually, for his mother kept returning, like a pernicious weed, even after he'd cut it down and cut it down some more.

You love your mother. Right? And you love your father. If love means thinking about. If love means having been raised by. If love means we are part of each other.

15. To find a secret garden amid it all, and to pick three golden apples.

Mostly his labors were internal. Certainly that was so with the three golden apples. No, the boy didn't have to *literally* pick three golden apples from his mother's secret fucking garden. His mother didn't have a secret garden, for one thing—or if she did, he didn't want to know about it. In fact, on drunken horrible nights, it seemed quite likely his mother *wanted* him to know about her secret garden, that this was where the drunken rambling was going, the tears about his father's latest dalliances, the staring from her chaise lounge by the pool. Even the best alcohol in the world—which they were drinking, a savagely expensive tequila, like no Mexican peasant had ever tasted—could make him feel better, could take the tarnish off the ghastly Southern gothic scene. In the actual South, the vines and the mulberry and the nightshade and the cuckoo insects and the crimes of passion and the ghosts from the Civil War provided some kind of hyperreality and context. Here, the watery look in his mother's eye, the soft fall of her robe against her unfortunately exposed thigh, had nothing to dim it, nothing to soften the blood-ridiculousness of it, the nightmare. And so Harry stumbled back to his room in the mansion, like a cave or prison, and turned on his music and tried to pound his way into oblivion.

It would be better if he didn't live with them, clearly. It was as if he were simultaneously expected to perform great feats and relinquish his own destiny.

Three little apples. Golden ones. Three is a magic number. (But there were four in this family—there was Laurabell. But she seemed so removed, at her young age, from all the ranting and raving, the terrible smear between mother-lover and son-husband. Here came a spill of poison in his gut. No escape, no escape for her either!) But three. The number must mean something in and of itself. Three: an unstable number, yet also the number of legs required for a stool to remain upright. It seemed to Harry that everything resorted to three after not too long. Although, he wanly speculated further, two was also a magical number. Or could be. As in: Harry and Cindy.

After his seasonal job at the racetrack, Harry had felt a little boost, a sense that a world was out there, that he could take brief forays into it, even if he did, at the end, come home. Nonetheless, he was woefully underprepared for life off the mount. His job just confirmed this. What to do? Surely being charming at parties couldn't be put on his résumé (not that he was all that charming, anyway).

One morning in the sunny kitchen, Zero was sitting at the island, staring at his phone. Hanna stood before the counter, looking at a recipe (she was planning the menu for a dinner party). Her phone rang and she started talking, quite loudly, as she always did into the phone. Zero gave her a nasty look, and she waltzed out of the room. Harry opened the refrigerator and closed it again. He sat down at the table.

"Dad, what you did with Cindy? How could you do that? On Easter. The girl I brought over as my date. To me, that's a really fucked-up message. For me, your son."

Zero squinted at him. Maybe he couldn't make him out very well with the sun streaming in. Maybe Harry was just a silhouette. "Harry, you're right, and I'm sorry. You shouldn't have had to see that. That was a mistake." Zero looked back down at his phone.

Harry sat, bathed in beams of light. He felt weak and tired.

"Is that it?"

Zero reluctantly broke from his screen, his head popping up as if it had snapped a thin string. "What do you want me to say, son?"

"I want, I want some acknowledgment. I mean, Cindy—she was the first girl I'd ever brought over here. This is my life. I'm trying to make a life."

"Yes, you're trying to make a life. About time, I'd say. And exactly how hard *are* you trying? How long can you coast on the poor son routine, this damaged-goods mama's boy role you've taken on?"

"I'm not a mama's boy," said Harry, his voice sounding wildly tinny and small. My God, his mother was virtually out to get him! If this were what being a mama's boy was like, he'd hate to be on her bad side! She was his active enemy. And yet everything she did for him, every single thing, was supposedly for his own good. Designed to make him strong, to overcome. And the tests kept coming, and she seemed, he thought in the recesses of his soul, to relish them.

"Let's talk specifics, Harry. Enough is enough. Are you ready to make some use of your college degree? I'm giving you the chance. I'm giving you *another* chance, for fuck's sake. Come work for me. No more fucking around with the racehorses and the shamans your mother loves so much."

"I do not want to work at Raytheon," said Harry, standing. "I will never work at Raytheon."

His father's face was pink but still handsome. His baldness oiled up, the glasses with puce rectangular frames—very au courant overall. Zero's mouth pursed, yet his eyes held no discernable feeling.

Harry steadied himself. He had come from this place, from these people, but he had the power to go somewhere on his own. To be his own person.

Ah, that would be the hardest task of all—if he could even manage it. Harry backed away from his father and started walking out of the kitchen.

He paused at the fruit bowl on the counter. The oranges and reds and yellows were brilliant against the black marble and shimmered in the morning light. The glow was misty and powdery, as if the fruit was unreal. Harry felt bold, as if his actions were simultaneously foretold and filled with freedom. He selected one apple, and then a second, and then a third one.

16. To go to the underworld, and to capture the dog, and to bring him home.

Sometimes when Harry was drifting toward sleep, an image of the music teacher came to him. His hair was thin and inert, like pencil lines around his face. His eyes were not kind and they were not unkind. Behind his glasses, they were simply still—and they remained still and clear and tranquil until those last agonized moments, when they beseeched Harry for help, when they wanted, above all, *life!* Everyone said it wasn't Harry's fault, but Harry had taken the blame regardless. Blame attached itself to him like an animal skin.

When the music teacher died, his hair hung forward over his cheekbones and blood came out of his mouth. The autopsy showed that it was an epileptic fit, and that Harry's harsh E-flat had nothing to do with it. Still, Harry could not get over his possible role in the man's death. Nor could his parents. Zero and Hanna found it to be a blotch. They covered it up.

In his room, Harry moved as if he were underwater. A leather suitcase lay open on the bed, as well as his gym bag. He packed his tennis racquet and his athletic shorts. He packed his polo shirts, his socks, his boxers. He packed his deodorant and his yearbooks. He packed a framed picture of his grandmother plus a folder of other photographs and memorabilia. He packed a box full of sci-fi and an art history textbook. He packed his camera and trophies from swim team.

He left the bedding, never his in the first place: sheets with fine black stitching, a gray chenille throw, a plaid comforter. He left his lamp, his dresser, a few pairs of shoes, his barbells, his old *Road & Track* and *Sports Illustrated* magazines. When he had sorted out almost everything, by the time he'd found his basketball in the back of the closet, Harry's eyes were blurred with tears. He had left before, for instance when he went to college, but never with this exact same sense: the sense that he might not come back, ever. It was a bitter feeling. His own mother. His own father. Why hadn't they been different? Why had they grown tentacles like squid, why were they in his business? Why couldn't they remain distinct, instead of ballooning out, smearing on everything? Why were they shapeshifters, why were they manipulators, why did they know everyone in town? It could have been different. He knew now that it could have been different.

Harry himself had died. But he would return to life, carrying what was left of who he had been.

17. And thusly for your mother once again to attempt, with renewed fervor, to make you insane.

Because she didn't want him to leave. They were in the driveway. Harry's eyes had dried by now. *You are mine, you are mine, you are mine,* it was as if she were chanting. Harry shook his head, trying to get the CD stand in the back of the Subaru. She stood behind him. "But why now? Why?" implored Hanna. Hesitation welled up in Harry; it wracked his nervous system like faulty penicillin. "I just have to, that's all," he said.

She would always be there. He knew she was everywhere. As she spoke to her friends around the pool, or the rent-a-disciples at Dr. Eurosmith's seminars, she would speak of him, and she'd create a narrative that she herself would feature in, and he would be, from now until the end of time, running around doing her errands. His father would be out fucking around, puffing up his chest and pretending none of it mattered, oblivious to what Harry might be feeling. Simply put, Harry had to get out of here! And yet it was probably the hardest thing he'd ever done. Harder than slaying a hundred-headed hydra. Harder than tricking Atlas into holding up the world. Harder than shoveling shit. Harder than wrestling a wild boar.

"Who do you think you are?" she was saying. "Have you no humility, no gratitude? We made you. We made you who you are."

Harry looked at his mother standing in the driveway, her arms wrapped around her own body, eyes shining with tears. Inside, his father was taking a shower.

18. And it's not so, if you happened to think it was over.

Was the last task to teach humility, or to be humiliating? He was to serve three years as a slave to a queen, who would dress him as a woman and make him sew with her. Indeed, Harry might have enjoyed sewing, or wearing something other than polo shirts and khakis. But there was no such queen, and there would be no dressing as a woman. Instead, alone in a rented guesthouse in Sam Hughes, Harry found that the button to his shorts was dangling, and so—another first in a year of them—he had to sew it back on. He bought a travel-size sewing kit at the pharmacy and arranged the needle, thread, scissors, and shorts around him on the couch. He snipped off the loose button and teased the stray threads out of the fabric. He put the button on the coffee table. He picked up the spool and let it tumble in his hand, and then he snipped the thread to length, and directed one end into the needle's eye. He got it on the first try (lucky!). He pulled the thread through, knotted the two ends together, and pulled them taut. He picked up the button again and aligned it on the fabric. When the button was firmly sewn, he snipped the thread and made another knot. He put away all his supplies and folded his shorts and placed them on the table and sat back on his new little couch, and he felt glad.

The refrigerator was filled with food he had picked out on his own. He did not yet have a job, but he had a few applications out.

19. To fight a river god, to marry, to marry again, to nearly die, to win a mother's love, to conquer the world ultimately, and to become a kind of god, too. Not exactly in that order, but the story does have to end.

At night, Harry lay in his small bedroom, letting the light of the moon wash in. The air conditioner was loud, like something was taking off in the closet, a spaceship grinding between sputter and glide. It was sometimes louder than the argument in his head. Those first few nights he had trouble sleeping. *To be a pawn* was a phrase that kept coming back to him. In the morning, he made coffee with his new coffeemaker, and he checked his phone. Usually the phone had no messages. Correction: always.

On his first Sunday morning in the bungalow, someone rang his doorbell. It was his neighbor, an old man. "We've lost our cat. He's on the roof and won't come back," said the man. He wouldn't look at Harry directly, but instead looked at the doorframe. He was trembling with anxiety. He was in his pajamas.

"I'll be right there, sir," said Harry. "I can help."

Harry put on his sandals and followed the man outside. A tiger cat was on the roof of the next house over, as he had said. It was walking along the side of the gutter. As they watched, it almost lost its balance, and the old man cried "Sonny!" Harry could see now that it was mewing. It was a very small cat.

Harry felt strong. He strode over to the Dumpster near the back of the house and jumped up on it. He stepped onto the cement block wall, and he reached over and catapulted himself onto the roof. The old man and his wife were arm in arm, huddled together in the driveway. Harry stood to full height and waved at them. The cat watched Harry with some suspicion, but not without hope.

Cerberus

The marriage had been going along just fine until Cerberus came along. Yes, the two young people had been together for three virtually blissful years, and it really looked like, sexual dysfunction aside, they were more or less meant for each other.

It felt like fate. Dusk had fallen by the time Mary and Kyle came out of the grocery store, their festive reusable bags filled with frozen entrées, overly spiced tapenades, and faux microbrewery beer. The sprawlscape surrounding them: a boarded-up brick building that used to be an Italian grocery, a supposed spa that could just as well have been a front for prostitution or an art gallery, a U.S. Postal Service administration building where mental-patient murderers were being groomed for later success in their inevitable life acts, a McDonald's with a dinosaur out front. They trundled past a dozen empty handicapped spots on their way to their Honda Civic, parked dangerously close to a couple of abandoned carts. Kyle clicked open the trunk. That's when they noticed the little monster of a dog, maybe part pit bull, or part boxer. He was sitting by one of the carts, shivering in the heat.

"Oh, look at that dog," said Mary, stopping in her tracks.

"Hey, pooch," said Kyle.

They furrowed their brows. The rough-and-tumble hound was looking at them, ears up like starched hankies, head cocked. He had sorrowful black eyes and a majestic jaw and neck. Probably weighed fifty or sixty pounds. Everything about him said *mutt* in the best possible way. He was a long-suffering brindled hero who cared deeply about people, was loyal as anything, but also had a mind of his own. He had a mission. His mission currently being foiled, it seemed, by sweeping abject loss. He had no collar.

He kept shivering, even with his cocked head, and now the slowly thumping tail on the asphalt.

★

Who knows why they brought him home? Something had been missing, but more to the point they were both kindhearted. The city's animal control people ("officers" being too noble a term) were foul sadistic pirates, lurking in white trucks behind buildings to net or rope any animal without representation. The holding facility was truly a pure and absolute hell. Kyle and Mary would have guessed this, but Mary had it confirmed a couple of months ago when she went there with a friend to look for the friend's lost dog. Poor little Chloe had gone missing and never returned. Every day on her way to work, Mary still saw the sign Marjorie had duct-taped to a pole at Fifth and Alvernon. It was fading and ripped now, as if someone had intentionally trashed the photocopied picture of the overweight and undersized beagle, swallowed up by the underground.

Cerberus had definitely escaped death, whether it was in that low-ceilinged, murder-scented facility, or in his life on the lam, trotting between Dumpsters behind the grocery stores and fast-food joints. Mary and Kyle stared at the dog, now in their living room, chewing industriously on an elongated rubber chicken.

"He's so cute," said Mary, hands limp on either side of her body. She was helpless in the face of this much cuteness, this much potential rescue.

"I know." Kyle leaned toward the dog. "Hey, pooch. Hey."

Cerberus stopped his chewing long enough to raise his head and take a short, meditative look at the outstretched hand.

That first evening, Kyle had an idea. It came out of something he'd seen on Animal Planet—that dog trainer, the super clean-cut, polo-shirt dude, midway between a marine and a dance instructor? That guy knew what he was talking about. For sure Kyle didn't—the only other dog trainer he remembered was his neighbor growing up, a lady who raised German shepherds. She was a mean one, her hair streaked and frayed at the ends, eyes always looking away when she spoke, surveying the vicinity for dog activity. It was uncertain what she did to make those dogs behave, but behave they did, and two or three times a year she sold AKC-registered puppies. Kyle's mother had been allergic to everything—everything! They didn't have any *plants*, let alone collies or even hamsters.

When Cerberus trotted from his spot on the rug, where he'd been gnawing the rubber chicken, over to Kyle's basket of biking gear, Kyle was initially dumbstruck, then said, "No, shit, oh shit, stay away from that,

Jesus, dog!" and lumbered over there, laughing. Cerberus let him take the first kneepad out of his mouth, but then he lunged for the other (still in the basket). Kyle tried to tug the thing from the dog's jaws, but Cerberus held on. He looked up with his beautiful black eyes and decided something—this is what Kyle thought later—then yanked the kneepad out of Kyle's hand with a gleeful ripping motion and trotted with it back toward the couch. The dog settled in near Mary, his tail slowly beating the rug.

"Shit," said Kyle.

"Look what the little doggy brought me," said Mary. "One of your kneecaps."

"Not my kneecap," said Kyle. "Look, I've still got both knees." He shook his leg at her, as if they were doing the hokey pokey.

"It's Kyle's little knee paddy-waddy," she said to the dog, now shaking the kneepad back and forth, gnawing, making a kind of *rrr—rrr—num* sound.

"He can't eat my shit, Mary. Man. Do you think this dog is trained?"

"He sat for us, didn't he? And he shook hands. This dog is so smart," she said in a normal voice, and then, in her new not-normal voice, gazing at the dog, "I'm in love with you, little dog."

Kyle frowned. It was all percolating by then: the puppy-mill woman and her stealthy commando approach to dog training. . . . the shepherds in their chain link kennels . . . the ballroom instructor dude on TV. Ballroom instructor dude said he believed in three things: love, discipline, and constancy. Constancy was a weird one. When he discussed constancy on the show, he was always sitting in a mint-green room on a Sam Levitz–type fake Zen couch, greenery whooshing away behind him in the window. Love was a given, a crowd pleaser. Everyone wanted to love his damn dog. Right? Obviously. You think of yourself as the kind of person who loves your dog. It was discipline, the middle word, squeezed in there like a laser beam. Now *that* was the important thing to remember, Kyle began to think, Cerberus chewing away.

They put signs up around the neighborhood, or Mary did. She ended up putting one on the pole with Chloe's sign still on it. Mary taped back together her friend's ripped and faded sign, though it seemed close to beyond hope in every way, BEAGLE—FEMALE—3 YEARS OLD— NEEDS MEDS! in block letters over a photo of Chloe on her dog bed. At the top of her sign, Marjorie had written GENEROUS REWARD, and at the bottom, BIG $$$$$. Mary taped her sign underneath: DOG FOUND

10/2—PIT BULL MIX?—BROWN & WHITE MALE—FOUND ALBERTSON'S/TANQUE VERDE—FRIENDLY. With Kyle's phone number. A few other pet notices had been taped or staple-gunned to this pole, too. There was a cat. There was another dog from long ago.

If only the lost signs and the found signs could hook up, thought Mary, amateur theologian. She was twenty-seven, and the injustices of the world loomed large. It seemed she really ought to do something about her life—or perhaps life in general. She could make a difference, but she wasn't completely sure how. Hers was a classic case of paralysis: if you need to clean the house, go to work, create a beauty package out of your own body, save your marriage, exercise and achieve overall personal wellness, learn Spanish, finally get to that treatise on violence by William Vollmann, create a family genealogy before your parents kicked it, et cetera, et cetera, then it was pretty difficult to gin up the energy to do anything at all except watch *Weeds* on cable. And so with the world. What was most important? Do you just pick a cause, any cause? How do you weigh every injustice's relative importance? Put Democrats in office, *check.* Save planet from sizzling up into a little sizzled French fry, *check.* Save the animals that were totally fucking being killed and dying, the single last *X* and *Y*, all the furry and fluffy and feathered things, just dying—poachers shooting the shit out of them for their left toenail, or pharmaceutical companies poisoning their water supply, or oil companies heaping oil on their red-feathered heads—it was all bad and they kept dying every damn day, *check.* People! People counted, too! People starving so their stomachs swelled, so they lost their minds, so they lost their children, *check.* People, take two, losing civil rights, women can't go to school, et cetera, et cetera, torture, really bad, extremely bad, war, all the wars, *check.* In any case, it was difficult to choose—let alone take in the gravity of any given problem. But then here came this dog out of nowhere, finding *her.* Finding them, she should say.

Her duty, though: try to find the little guy's rightful owner. So she'd braved getting out of the Civic (they couldn't afford a Prius) and casting her lot with the ephemera of abandoned pets gone by, losts and founds that didn't match up. She'd put up fifteen signs in all, and went to four veterinary clinics, too.

Two weeks, not one call. In the meantime, certain things did become clear. First of all, they had to find something to call him. They fooled around with various names, finally coming up with "Cerberus." It was Kyle's idea—he'd always had a crush on his high school English teacher and he'd gotten double credit or something like that on his *Odyssey* poster.

Either they were lucky or the dog was super smart, because he responded to the name right away.

They agreed on the name, and they agreed that Cerberus smiled so sweetly. It wasn't much longer before Mary and Kyle took down the signs. They bought a collar, a leash, and two real dog bowls. They put his picture on the fridge and on Facebook. They offered him treats and toys, and soon enough he had a basketful of rubber and rope playthings in the living room.

Cerberus was a watcher, a secret watcher, always aware of exactly where Mary and Kyle were in the house or yard. He preferred to lie in a place where he could see the two of them at once, and if they were in separate parts of the house, he positioned himself equidistant between them. The vet said he was about eighteen months, maybe two years old. He'd broken a leg once and it hadn't healed properly—a minor break, but it looked (from the X-ray) that it had never been set. That was why, when he was tired, he had a small limp. He was a laid-back eater, which seemed to indicate that he might not have been on his own for too long, that hunger wasn't a fear for him. At night, he lay on the rug by their bed. It was only after they'd torn down the signs and bought the dog dishes that he jumped on the couch. He also commandeered the La-Z-Boy Kyle's mother had given them.

Kyle and Mary swapped off walking Cerberus in the mornings, though Kyle did it more often. He was an early riser anyway, and before Cerberus, he'd used the first hour of the day for his own work before going to the office. They used a Gentle Leader collar, a loop around the snout, like Marjorie had used with Chloe. They also used a "clicker"—another of Marjorie's ideas. You click it and give the dog a treat when he obeys a command. Sit. Click. Treat. The dog associates the click noise with the treat, apparently.

"Look, Mary, I don't know about this. The guy on TV? He wasn't all clicking the dog. Anyway, it seems redundant. Why click the clicker when you're giving the treat? The dog's already associating good behavior with a treat, so why the middle man?"

"For one thing, you can eventually stop giving him the treat this way. Like, the click becomes the treat."

"Why would you want to do that?"

Mary was looking down at Cerberus, lying on the kitchen floor as if he'd been shot. "Well, in case you don't have any treats, for instance. Or if he was fat."

"Yeah, like Chloe."

"Don't talk trash about Chloe."

"I'm not. She was fat, though."

"That's because she was smart enough to find the dog food in the garage."

"I thought it was because Marjorie was a pushover."

"Kyle, dogs are aural. The click lodges in their brains. I don't know why."

"Well, the dude on TV, he was like—don't you remember that show? He had a system: love, discipline, constancy."

"Love, discipline, constancy?"

"Yeah."

"What the fuck is constancy?"

"Constancy is eating Trader Joe's spaghetti three times a week."

Big glare from Mary.

Kyle: "Kidding! It's like, don't change how you do crap. No chaos for the little hound dog. Just do the same thing all the time."

"That's a weird motto, I think."

"Whatever. The guy's a billionaire now. Love, discipline, constancy."

"Instead of that capitalist bullshit dominance routine, we should use rewards, the positive reinforcement system. The clicker underscores that."

"The clicker's super stupid," said Kyle.

"At least give it a try! Marjorie thought it was awesome, it completely worked for her."

"Marjorie has lost touch with reality."

"The approach works. It just takes patience, is all."

Kyle shrugged, having been overcome by torpor and ennui. "I'm just saying. Like what the guy on TV says. So what's for dinner, anyway?"

Mary looked neutral to marginally forgiving. "I don't know. Spaghetti?"

Their neighborhood was a 1950s development of adobe brick one-story homes, third of an acre lots. Although they walked the dog separately most of the time, Mary and Kyle both took the same route: left out of the driveway, left on Leonora, up six blocks to Eighth Street, left on Eighth, left on Chantilly, back down six blocks to round out your circle, left on Sixth, and then home.

While walking Cerberus the next morning, Kyle tried to conjure up the TV guy. By discipline, he didn't mean *hit* the dog—not that Kyle would ever hit the dog. Though maybe he'd shove the dog, if he had to. He did more or less swat the dog's head when he was trying to retrieve his biking glove from his jaws. Was a swat a hit? Was a shove a hit? Yeah, a swat was a hit, Kyle knew. A shove was a fucking hit, too.

Kyle's dad had let him know what a hit was, no ambiguity there.

But the TV guy. The TV guy just entered the room and stood there regally, with his polo shirt tucked in and absolutely no sense of humor, and the dog (and the nice lady owner) suddenly acted ultra docile. Oh yeah, the TV guy made some kind of *spriiittt* or *splik* or *spluuff* sound, too.

"*Spriiittt*," Kyle said on the corner of Leonora and Eighth, looking down at Cerberus. The clicker remained in his pocket, unused.

Cerberus did not look up. His was an attitude of relaxation, tail gently wagging, nose pointed toward a yard where the homeowners had added three berms, or what might have been berms in Scotland, but here looked like piles of gravel with a couple of random plants stuck on top.

"Cerberus!"

The dog was viewing, perhaps, a plastic bag stuck in the bougainvillea.

"Cerberus! *Spriiittt*!"

Cerberus looked up at Kyle. He sat down. Fucking brilliant! This was totally working.

Kyle and Mary had gotten married at La Paloma, a resort up in the Foothills. It had been funny, their courtship. They were, as they liked to put it, *best friends*. They enjoyed sex—who didn't enjoy sex?—but both individually and together they'd acknowledged concern about the sex life aspect of this union. Probably the sex life aspect was what kept them from getting engaged for so long, for the five years they were first dating and then living together before he popped the question. Time and again they'd gotten close to this point, and time and again one or the other had pivoted and run the other direction. First Kyle was ready. He began talking about his grandmother's property in Wisconsin, about how he'd always thought he and his sister might buy it someday and fix it up and make it a summer place for the new generation to come. The way he said "new generation": hesitant and a little breathless, not looking at Mary directly. Eventually Mary's lack of enthusiasm—she just never picked up the thread—got to him. He retreated, and that's when his obsession with billiards kicked in. The next year was her turn. It all started at his sister's wedding. Maybe it was because she had her period and was also getting over a cold, but Mary felt receptive to everything that night: the music, the dress, the intoxicating words of promise. She and Kyle got smashed and slow-danced up a storm, his mother regarding them stealthily, like prey. Mary was thinking: Sigh. She was thinking: Circle of Life. Kyle's heart began to beat a little faster, he started thinking again about the house in Wisconsin—and it was almost as if Mary were clairvoyant, the fine-tuning, the accuracy of her realization—and she freaked. She jumped up from her chair of soft edges and turned the other direction posthaste. *Oh shit, let's just live together!*

That flip-flop happened at least twice more. One careless day, they both landed on the marriage square at the same time, and that's when he asked the question, and that's when yes was her answer.

They even joked about it, The Problem. As with the desire to get married, each took the blame for the lackluster sex life him- or herself for a time, and then tossed it to the other person. And life went on. And sex was had. It was like a rusted-out but still-functioning Toyota Corolla. It did run; it just wasn't a glam car.

"Maybe I remember it wrong," said Kyle. "Maybe it's assertive, patient, consistent."

"That guy is so full of shit," said Mary, sitting on the bed with her laptop. She was online, checking out why Cher's daughter was depressed.

"No, he's got it down. You have to be assertive, right? You're the dominant animal. You're the lead animal in the pack. You've got to keep cool, no matter what. And of course, consistent. That makes sense. It goes with patient. You just do the same thing all the time, again and again and again. You just keep doing it. You do it forever. Know what I mean?"

Mary gave Kyle a forbearing look. "I can't really see the assertive part."

He shrugged and went back into the living room.

Cerberus was sitting on the La-Z-Boy. It was a little worse for wear, the chair, since he'd eaten one of the arms. All Kyle could hear was Cerberus's quiet panting.

Mary popped out of the bedroom. She had tears in her eyes.

"What is a dog, Kyle? What do you think a dog is?"

"A dog. What? Um, a dog is just god spelled backward."

Kyle was lying supine on the couch. He had tried to get the cushion right under his head, but it was eluding him.

"A dog is just the stupid-ass word we put on this creature. This creature here. An animal, like us. A being. A *being*, Kyle. What bullshit it all is, discipline, assertion, chew toys. Assertiveness, affection, playtime. Happy days, sad days, chew toys. Is this how you want to live?" Her voice rose shrilly at the end.

Kyle sat up and threw the cushion on the rug. "Like the whole gentle love approach is working. No—fucking *not*."

"Like you've given it a chance."

"Go on, love that puppy up, Mary. Dog chews the leg off the dresser—give him a ham bone. Why? Because the dog has stopped chewing. Of course, there's no more dresser, but whatever. What matters is the dog is getting rewarded for not doing something. But the problem is the *not doing* is linked completely to the *doing*. See? The doing and the not doing, same deal. If the dog didn't do, he couldn't stop doing. So he's getting the damn ham bone for doing."

Mary was shaking her head, dry-eyed now. "God. God!"

"Dog spelled backward," said Kyle, pointing at her with a Vegas flourish. He picked up the cushion, pitched it to the other end of the couch, and repositioned himself in that direction, falling like a tree. "I'm napping."

Kyle went online to clarify the triumvirate of secrets held by the possibly gay (he now thought) ex-marine dog trainer, and found out it was actually exercise, discipline, affection—a little dubious, thought Kyle, who had gotten attached first to love, discipline, constancy, and then to assertive, patient, consistent. It was all beginning to remind him of a "What Doesn't Belong?" picture in a kid's book, much as Mary had suggested, not like he'd tell her he agreed.

Cat, kitten, wastebasket.

Summer home, Kyle, Mary.

It didn't finally matter, because you just had to have a system—and stick to it, for fuck's sake—so Kyle had, at least, taken to making the *spriiittt* sound with increasing, Darth Vader–like authority. Sometimes Mary came across her husband standing with his arms crossed, glaring at the corner of the room—waiting for the dog to sit or whatever.

"What next, Kyle? Make him wait while you eat your waffle in the morning?"

"I'm the big dog around here," Kyle said half-jokingly.

By now, Mary had tapped into a whole network of reward-based trainers, thanks to beagle-free Marjorie. They'd had coffee at Starbucks one morning, and Marjorie's eyes had welled with tears as she leaned over her no-whip caramel macchiato. "All I remember is the time I spanked poor Chloe, spanked her little rear end because she'd burrowed a hole into the back of my Restoration Hardware couch, you know? I'd just gotten it, like, six months before. The poor little dog, she gave me this look I'll never forget—like I'd betrayed her. And now I'd do anything in the world to get her back and take back that moment, take back that time I hurt her."

Marjorie was twirling her hair frantically with her finger.

"It's okay, Marjorie. She knew you loved her, I know she did," Mary said, reaching across the table and squeezing her friend's (other) hand, and in her mind promising herself she'd never, ever make that same mistake. Marjorie's views on dog training were expounded upon and shored up by the women at Caring Partners. The manager there, an older woman with a deep and unusually animated voice, said you must not in any way, shape, or form make the dog feel pain. If you did, you were a torturer, a fiend, and a petite dictator. She was a bit over the top, but what she said made sense. Who would strike a friend (a "Caring Partner")? The Gentle Leader was the only collar they condoned for walking the dog, "though with the right kind of training he won't need a leash at all."

Cerberus, sitting on the living room rug, the rug only slightly frayed at the edge where he had ripped off the tassels; Cerberus, whose Gentle Leader collar was the only thing standing between him and unchecked leash pulling, who had destroyed three shoes, one kneepad, a chair, and a cabinet panel, and who seemed oblivious to all training methods equally—was no longer just a mottled, motley stray with a happy expression and a large open mouth, but a battleground.

It was the week before Thanksgiving when Mary, walking Cerberus early in the morning, saw a coyote. Cerberus saw the coyote, too, and the coyote saw Cerberus.

Kyle had gotten back into billiards, and he'd gone out the previous night until rather late, so she'd taken the initiative and stumbled out of bed at six-thirty to walk the dog. For the first few blocks, Cerberus had been on his best behavior. Straining the leash a bit maybe, but overall willing to walk alongside Mary with a confident stride, swept up in the world's opportunity.

They were four blocks away from the house, and Mary had just picked up Cerberus's business with a blue waste pickup bag, flipping it inside out and knotting it so she didn't have to touch the contents. This time of year, mornings were cool, lovely actually, the neighborhood quiet and still. Mary was about to walk into the alley to drop the bag into the Dumpster when she saw the coyote. He was thin, his fur white, gray, and tan, but mostly white—he was a ghostly image overall. The coyote's ears were pointed and his snout was long. There was no wise-wolf look happening, but he didn't look stupid either. He looked wild. She thought: Wow. She thought: Weirdly chilling and ghostly, and I don't completely know what's going on.

Cerberus was at full attention. His ears were no longer adorable folded napkins. He stood still, but Mary sensed action brewing inside him. His body seemed rooted to the ground, and fleetingly Mary thought of the word *grounded*, how this word could really feel.

"Come on, Cerberus, let's go," she said under her breath, half turning and pulling at the Gentle Leader. Gently, yes, but not leading after all. Cerberus would not move. He began to growl.

The coyote was standing sideways to them, gazing with his head turned. Cerberus lunged. The Gentle Leader being all of a sudden fucking useless. The leash slipped out of Mary's grasp before she even knew what was happening, and there went Cerberus, running toward the coyote. The coyote hunched, skittered three feet back and sideways, and then faced Cerberus head on. The dog was growling, the coyote staring at him with concentration, and Mary thought about how coyotes never get Tender Chunks of Lamb with Gravy or Science Diet Large Dog Nuggets, nor bowls of water with ice cubes, nor rubber chickens, but had to kill beagles and cats. It happened all the time. You'd come across a patch of fur on the road, or hear a neighbor's plaintive call, "Fluffy! Fluffy!" Then silence. Fluffy no more.

The two animals circled each other in fits and starts, a kind of tango.

"Cerberus, come back. *Cerberus!*"

The coyote bolted. The coyote was gone.

Cerberus ran in the wild dog's shadow, up past the back gates of at least two houses, past an electrical box bolted into the ground, past a tall prickly pear cactus and a scrawny palo verde and a willow acacia and another Dumpster. He turned past a wall and Mary was still shouting, and she couldn't see him anymore.

Kyle was still in bed when he heard Mary, distantly, as if in a dream. It took him a moment to register, and then he bolted up and ran barefoot out of the house. Out to the street Kyle jogged, and when he looked east, he saw Mary four houses down, talking to a neighbor. It appeared to be a hurried and heated exchange, a botched relay. When she saw him, she came running. "Cerberus got away. He chased a coyote. In the alley. Now he's gone."

"Which way did he run? Are *you* okay?"

"I'm fine!" shrieked Mary.

Kyle ran into the house to put on his shoes and then went back outside. Mary said she'd go to the schoolyard and the arroyo. He'd take the alleys. He hurried through the no-man's land between his property and the neighbor's, started marching down the dusty alley behind their house. A coyote—wow. Kyle had grown up in Cincinnati. There was something incredible about this, it was story worthy—as long as they found Cerberus and everything was all right in the end. Kyle almost shouted when he saw two dogs near Leonora, but they were just the old lady's dogs from the end of the street, a Doberman mix and a white poodle. They must have gotten out the back gate.

Walking up another alley, Kyle worked through potential next steps. Call the pound? Put up one of those damn signs again? This time for a dog lost, not found. He had his collar and even his leash on, Mary had said, so it would be obvious he belonged to someone. It should be okay, unless he got hit by a car—the dog had shown no sense when it came to traffic. Mary would not sleep nor eat nor smile until they got him back, this Kyle knew, a dull tickle at the back of his neck. He didn't even consider what would happen if the dog and the coyote got into a fight.

Five blocks away, Mary's body was filled with rage and conviction. The world was wholly unfair, God was an asshole, and the setup in general, the way it was with animals, the way her own life was, the way it was at work, the way it was with Kyle, the reasons they came to Tucson, the family history she seemed to be mired in, the half-assed way she'd participated in just about everything, the whole kit was jerry-rigged, fucked up, and set to fail. It had been so beautiful when they'd found the dog, a sign even. And now the dog had gotten away—she'd let the dog go, she was to blame—and everything was ruined. She ran haphazardly around the perimeter of the school, looking into nooks, places coyotes might hide. Screaming her dog's name, as if she could summon him from the air.

Fluffy, Fluffy, Fluffy no more. Mary and Kyle sat in their living room after their search for Cerberus failed. They both felt hung over from stress (in Kyle's case, also beer). They'd called Pima Animal Care Center—the maligned men who might now be their saviors. Mary was scared they'd put Cerberus to sleep accidently—or if he hurt someone. Kyle was having no thoughts. His brain: empty.

They walked around the neighborhood twice more that day, knocking on doors up and down their street and the next. Mary called PACC four times. She didn't call Marjorie.

In the dead of night, Kyle and Mary made love. Darkness folded over them like a velvet curtain. Sometimes a breeze lifted the fabric and stars shone in the distance. Mary cried. Kyle touched his hand to her face, carried wetness on his knuckle to his side of the bed. They both stayed awake, listening for coyote yips. The world felt hollow and rich.

Cerberus imagined he was at the center of the universe. He had a dream of lying on a rug in a bedroom, two people asleep on a risen mattress. They snuggled up, while he had to create his own circle of warmth. It was early morning, and soon one of them would get up to walk him. There was the one with the high voice and trembling hand. There was the one who talked on the phone and laughed, staring out toward the mountains. Cerberus dreamed he was in the middle of the earth, and he had a job to do. His job was to let the world in, let in all the birdsong and the yips and howls. In the dream, Cerberus was confused and afraid, because all this time he'd thought his job was to keep those things out.

Mary woke first in the morning. The radio alarm came on—chatter, some bad news she couldn't identify. She turned it off, got out of bed, and headed toward the bathroom. If he were here, Cerberus would have leapt to his feet, and she'd pat his head and whisper something. He'd listen while she was in the bathroom, and then follow her down the hall after she'd dressed, wait as she gathered the implements: Gentle Leader, leash, clicker, fanny bag of dog treats, waste bag. But when she got out of the bathroom, it was only Kyle in the room, a sleeping giant. She walked to the kitchen and stared out.

Cerberus's dream swept over him like a shadow. His paws tensed and jumped under his head. He opened his eyes, shivered. He knew he had to keep them safe.

Safe meant alive.

He would keep them safe, before long.

Acknowledgments

Grateful acknowledgment is made to the following publications, in which these stories originally appeared: "Orange Blossoms" in *Alaska Quarterly Review,* "Olympus Falls" and "The Three Graces" in *The Southern Review,* "Be Who You Are" in *Telling Stories Out of Court: Narratives about Women and Workplace Discrimination,* and "The Lotus Eaters" in *xo Orpheus: Fifty New Myths.* Thanks to those editors, and to my inimitable readers, Sylvia Brownrigg, Ann Cummins, Cecily Patterson, and Reed Karaim, as well as to the students in my fall 2009 novel workshop and Julie Hirsch: exceptional writing companions in this endeavor.

About the Author

AURELIE SHEEHAN is the author of two novels and two short story collections, most recently *Jewelry Box: A Collection of Histories*. Her short fiction has appeared in *Conjunctions*, *Fence*, *The Mississippi Review*, *The New England Review*, *Ploughshares*, and *The Southern Review*. She teaches fiction at the University of Arizona.